M        Rankin, Ian.
              Knots and crosses

M        Rankin, Ian.
              Knots and
          crosses

| DATE | ISSUED TO |
|------|-----------|
| OCT 1 1987 | 77-166 |
| OCT 6 1987 | 78-1086 |
| OCT 1 6 1987 | 77-178 |
| OCT 2 9 1987 | 77-116 |
| NOV 1 0 1987 | 77-166 |

*Knots and Crosses*

*by Ian Rankin*

KNOTS AND CROSSES

# Knots and Crosses

## IAN RANKIN

PUBLISHED FOR THE CRIME CLUB BY
DOUBLEDAY & COMPANY, INC.
GARDEN CITY, NEW YORK
1987

All of the characters in this book
are fictitious, and any resemblance
to actual persons, living or dead,
is purely coincidental.

M

Library of Congress Cataloging-in-Publication Data
Rankin, Ian.
Knots and crosses.
I. Title
PR6068.A57K6 1987 823'.914 87-5342
ISBN 0-385-24307-3
Copyright © 1987 by Ian Rankin
All Rights Reserved
Printed in the United States of America
*First Edition in the United States of America*

*To Miranda*
*without whom*
*nothing is worth finishing*

*Knots and Crosses*

# PROLOGUE

## I

The girl screamed once, only the once.

Even that, however, was a minor slip on his part. That might have been the end of everything, almost before it had begun. Neighbours inquisitive, the police called in to investigate. No, that would not do at all. Next time he would tie the gag a little tighter, just a little tighter, just that little bit more secure.

Afterwards, he went to the drawer and took from it a ball of string. He used a pair of sharp nail-scissors, the kind girls always seem to use, to snip off a length of about six inches, then he put the ball of string and the scissors back into the drawer. A car revved up outside, and he went to the window, upsetting a pile of books on the floor as he did so. The car, however, had vanished, and he smiled to himself. He tied a knot in the string, not any special kind of knot. There was an envelope lying ready on the sideboard.

## II

It was April 28th. Wet, naturally, the grass percolating water as John Rebus walked to the grave of his father, dead five years to the day. He placed a wreath so that it lay, yellow and red, the colours of remembrance, against the still shining marble. He paused for a moment, trying to think of things to say, but there seemed nothing to say, nothing to think. He had been a good enough father and that was that. The old man wouldn't have wanted him to waste his words in any case. So he stood there, hands respectfully behind his back, crows laughing on the walls around him, until the water seeping into his shoes told him that there was a warm car waiting for him at the cemetery gates.

He drove quietly, hating to be back here in Fife, back where the old days had never been "good old days," where ghosts rustled in the shells of empty houses and the shutters went up every evening on a handful of desultory shops, those metal shutters that gave the vandals somewhere to write their names. How Rebus hated it all, this singular lack of an environment. It stank the way it had always done: of misuse, of disuse, of the sheer wastage of life.

He drove the eight miles towards the open sea, to where his brother Michael still lived. The rain eased off as he approached the skull-grey coast, the car throwing up splashings of water from a thousand crevasses in the road. Why was it, he wondered, that they never seemed to fix the road here, while in Edinburgh they worked on the surface so often that things were made even worse? And why, above all, had he made the maniacal decision to come all the way through to Fife, just because it was the anniversary of the old man's death? He tried to focus his mind on something else, and found himself fantasising about his next cigarette.

Through the rain, falling as drizzle now, Rebus saw a girl about his daughter's age walking along the grass verge. He slowed the car, examined her in his mirror as he passed her, and stopped. He motioned for her to come to his window.

Her short breaths were visible in the cool, still air, and her dark hair fell in rats-tails down her forehead. She looked at him apprehensively.

"Where are you going, love?"

"Kirkcaldy."

"Do you want a lift?"

She shook her head, drops of water flying from her coiled hair.

"My mum said I should never accept lifts from strangers."

"Well," said Rebus, smiling, "your mum is quite right. I've got a daughter about your age and I tell her the same thing. But it *is* raining, and I *am* a policeman, so you can trust me. You've still got a fair way to go, you know."

She looked up and down the silent road, then shook her head again.

"Okay," said Rebus, "but take care. Your mum was quite right."

He wound his window up again and drove off, watching her in his mirror as she watched him. Clever kid. It was good to know that parents still had a little sense of responsibility left. If only the same could be said of his ex-wife. The way she had brought up their daughter was a disgrace. Michael, too, had given his daughter too long a leash. Who was to blame?

Rebus's brother owned a respectable house. He had followed in the old man's footsteps and become a stage hypnotist. He seemed to be quite good at it, too, from all accounts. Rebus had never asked Michael how it was done, just as he had never shown any interest or curiosity in the old man's act. He had observed that this still puzzled Michael, who would drop hints and red herrings as to the authenticity of his own stage act for him to chase up if he so wished.

But then John Rebus had too many things to chase up, and that had been the position during all of his fifteen years on the force. Fifteen years, and all he had to show were an amount of self-pity and a busted marriage with a innocent daughter hanging between them. It was more disgusting than sad. And meantime Michael was happily married with two kids and a larger house than Rebus could ever afford. He headlined at hotels, clubs, and even theatres as far away as Newcastle and Wick. Occasionally he would make six-hundred quid from a single show. Outrageous. He drove an expensive car, wore good clothes, and would never have been caught dead standing in the pissing rain in a graveyard in Fife on the dullest April day for many a year. No, Michael was too clever for that. And too stupid.

"John! Christ, what's up? I mean, it's great to see you. Why didn't you phone to warn me you were coming? Come on inside."

It was the welcome Rebus had expected: embarrassed surprise, as though it were painful to be reminded that one still had some family left alive. And Rebus had noted the use of the word "warn" where "tell" would have sufficed. He was a policeman. He noticed such things.

Michael Rebus bounded through to the living-room and turned down the wailing stereo.

"Come on in, John," he called. "Do you want a drink? Coffee perhaps? Or something stronger? What brings you here?"

Rebus sat down as though he were in a stranger's house, his back straight and professional. He examined the panelled walls of the room—a new feature—and the framed photographs of his niece and nephew.

"I was just in the neighbourhood," he said.

Michael, turning from the drinks cabinet with the glasses ready, suddenly remembered, or did a good impression of just having remembered.

"Oh, John, I forgot all about it. Why didn't you tell me? Shit, I hate forgetting about dad."

"Just as well you're a hypnotist then and not Mickey the Memory Man, isn't it? Give me that drink, or are you two getting engaged?"

Michael, smiling, absolved, handed over the glass of whisky.

"Is that your car outside?" asked Rebus, taking the glass. "I mean the big BMW?"

Michael, still smiling, nodded.

"Christ," said Rebus. "You treat yourself well."

"As well as I treat Chrissie and the kids. We're building an extension onto the back of the house. Somewhere to put a jacuzzi or a sauna. They're the in thing just now, and Chrissie's desperate to keep ahead of the field."

Rebus took a swallow of whisky. It turned out to be a malt. Nothing in the room was cheap, but none of it was exactly desirable either. Glass ornaments, a crystal decanter on a silver salver, the TV and video, the inscrutably miniature hi-fi system, the onyx lamp. Rebus felt a little guilty about that lamp. Rhona and he had given it to Michael and Chrissie as a wedding present. Chrissie no longer spoke to him. Who could blame her?

"Where is Chrissie, by the way?"

"Oh, she's out doing some shopping. She has her own car now. The kids will still be at school. She'll pick them up on the way home. Are you staying for something to eat?"

Rebus shrugged his shoulders.

"You'd be welcome to stay," said Michael, meaning that Rebus wouldn't. "So how's the cop-shop? Still muddling along?"

"We lose a few, but they don't get the publicity. We catch a few, and they do. It's the same as always, I suppose."

The room, Rebus was noticing, smelled of toffee-apples, of penny arcades.

Michael was speaking:

"This is a terrible business about those girls being kidnapped."

Rebus nodded.

"Yes," he said, "yes, it is. But we can't strictly call it kidnapping, not yet. There hasn't been a demand note or anything. It's more likely to be a straightforward case of sexual assault."

Michael stared up from his chair.

"Straightforward? What's straightforward about that?"

"It's just the terminology we use, Mickey, that's all." Rebus shrugged again and finished his drink.

"Well, John," said Michael, sitting, "I mean, we've both got daughters, too. You're so casual about the whole thing. I mean, it's frightening to think of it." He shook his head slowly in the world-wide expression of shared grief, and relief, too, that the horror was someone else's for the moment. "It's frightening," he repeated. "And in Edinburgh of all places. I mean, you never think of that sort of thing happening in Edinburgh, do you?"

"There's more happening in Edinburgh that anyone knows."

"Yes." Michael paused. "I was across there just last week playing at one of the hotels."

"You didn't tell me."

It was Michael's turn to shrug his shoulders.

"Would you have been interested?" he said.

"Maybe not," said Rebus, smiling, "but I would have come along anyway."

Michael laughed. It was the laughter of birthdays, of money found in an old pocket.

"Another whisky, sir?" he said.

"I thought you were never going to ask."

Rebus returned to his study of the room while Michael went to the cabinet.

"How's the act going?" he asked. "And I really *am* interested."

"It's going fine," said Michael. "In fact, it's going very well indeed. There's talk of a television spot, but I'll believe that when I see it."

"Great."

Another drink reached Rebus's willing hand.

"Yes, and I'm working on a new slot. It's a bit scary though." An inch of gold flashed on Michael's wrist as he tipped the glass to his lips. The watch was expensive: it had no numbers on its face. It seemed to Rebus that the more expensive something was, the less of it there always seemed to be: tiny little hi-fi systems, watches without numbers, the translucent Dior ankle socks on Michael's feet.

"Tell me about it," he said, taking his brother's bait.

"Well," said Michael, sitting forward in his chair, "I take members of the audience back into their past lives."

"Past lives?"

Rebus was staring at the floor as if admiring the design of the dark and light green carpet.

"Yes," Michael continued. "Reincarnation, born again, that

sort of thing. Well, I shouldn't have to spell it out to you, John. After all, *you're* the Christian."

"Christians don't believe in past lives, Mickey. Only future ones."

Michael stared at Rebus, demanding silence.

"Sorry," said Rebus.

"As I was saying, I tried the act out in public for the first time last week, though I've been practising it for a while with my private consultees."

"Private consultees?"

"Yes. They pay me money for private hypnotherapy. I stop them smoking, or make them more confident, or stop them from wetting the bed. Some are convinced that they have past lives, and they ask me to put them under so that they can prove it. Don't worry though. Financially, it's all above board. The tax-man gets his cut."

"And do you prove it? Do they have past lives?"

Michael rubbed a finger around the rim of his glass, now empty.

"You'd be surprised," he said.

"Give me an example."

Rebus was following the lines of the carpet with his eyes. Past lives, he thought to himself. Now there was a thing. There was plenty of life in *his* past.

"Well," said Michael, "remember I told you about my show in Edinburgh last week? Well," he leaned further forward in his chair, "I got this woman up from the audience. She was a small woman, middle-aged. She'd come in with an office-party. She went under pretty easily, probably because she hadn't been drinking as heavily as her friends. Once she was under, I told her that we were going to take a trip into her past, way, way back before she was born. I told her to think back to the earliest memory she had . . ."

Michael's voice had taken on a professional but easy mellifluence. He spread his hands before him as if playing to an audience. Rebus, nursing his glass, felt himself relax a little. He thought back to a childhood episode, a game of football, one brother pitted against the other. The warm mud of a July shower, and their mother, her sleeves rolled up, stripping them both and putting them, giggling knots of arms and legs, into the bath . . .

". . . well," Michael was saying, "she started to speak, and in a voice not quite her own. It was weird, John. I wish you *had* been there to see it. The audience were silent, and I was feeling all cold and then hot and then cold again, and it had nothing to do with the hotel's heating-system by the way. I'd done it, you see. I'd taken that woman into a past life. She was a nun. Do you believe that? A *nun.* And she said that she was alone in her cell. She described the convent and everything, and then she started to recite something in Latin, and some people in the audience actually *crossed* themselves. I was bloody well petrified. My hair was probably standing on end. I brought her out of it as quickly as I could, and there was a long pause before the crowd started to applaud. Then, maybe out of sheer relief, her friends started to cheer and laugh, and that broke the ice. At the end of the show, I found out that this woman was a staunch Protestant, a Rangers supporter no less, and she swore blind that she knew no Latin at all. Well, *somebody* inside her did. I'll tell you that."

Rebus was smiling.

"It's a nice story, Mickey," he said.

"It's the truth." Michael opened his arms wide in supplication. "Don't you believe me?"

"Maybe."

Michael shook his head.

"You must make a pretty bad copper, John. I had around a hundred and fifty witnesses. Iron-clad."

Rebus could not pull his attention away from the design in the carpet.

"Plenty of people believe in past lives, John."

*Past lives . . . Yes, he believed in some things . . . In God, certainly . . . But past lives . . .* Without warning, a face screamed up at him from the carpet, trapped in its cell.

He dropped his glass.

"John? Is anything wrong? Christ, you look as if you've seen . . ."

"No, no, nothing's the matter." Rebus retrieved the glass and stood up. "I just . . . I'm fine. It's just that," he checked his watch, a watch with numbers, "well, I'd better be going. I'm on duty this evening."

Michael was smiling weakly, glad that his brother was not going to stay, but embarrassed at his relief.

"We'll have to meet again soon," he said, "on neutral territory."

"Yes," said Rebus, tasting once again the tang of toffee-apples. He felt a little pale, a little shaky, as though he were too far out of his territory. "Let's do that."

Once or twice or three times a year, at weddings, funerals, or over the telephone at Christmas, they promised themselves this get-together. The mere promise now was a ritual in itself, and so could be safely proffered and just as safely ignored.

"Let's do that."

Rebus shook hands with Michael at the door. Escaping past the BMW to his own car, he wondered how alike they were, his brother and him. Uncles and aunts in their funeral-cold rooms occasionally commented, "Ah, you're both the spitting image of your mother." That was as far as it went. John Rebus knew that his own hair was a shade of brown lighter than Michael's, and that his eyes were a shade of green darker. He knew also, however, that the differences between them were such that any similarities were made to look unutterably superficial. They were brothers without any sense of brotherhood. Brotherhood belonged to the past.

He waved once from the car and was gone. He would be back in Edinburgh within the hour, and on duty another half-hour after that. He knew that the reason he could never feel comfortable in Michael's house was Chrissie's hatred of him, her unshakeable belief that he alone had been responsible for the break-up of his marriage. Maybe she was right at that. He tried ticking off in his mind the definite chores of the next seven or eight hours. He had to tidy up a case of burglary and serious assault. A nasty one that. The CID was undermanned as it was, and now these abductions would stretch them even more. Those two young girls, girls his own daughter's age. It was best not to think about it. By now they would be dead, or would wish that they were dead. God have mercy on them. In Edinburgh of all places, in his own dear city.

A maniac was on the loose.

People were staying in their homes.

*And a screaming in his memory.*

Rebus shrugged, feeling a silent sensation of attrition in one of his shoulders. It was not his business after all. Not yet.

Back in his living-room, Michael Rebus poured himself another whisky. He went to the stereo and turned it all the way up, then reached underneath his chair and, after a little fumbling, pulled out an ashtray that was hidden there.

# PART ONE

## *"There Are Clues Everywhere"*

### I

On the steps of the Great London Road police station in Edinburgh, John Rebus lit his last legitimate cigarette of the day before pushing open the imposing door and stepping inside.

The station was old, its floor dark and marbled. It had about it the fading grandeur of a dead aristocracy. It had character.

Rebus waved to the duty sergeant, who was tearing old pictures from the notice-board and pinning up new ones in their place. He climbed the great curving staircase to his office. Campbell was just leaving.

"Hello, John."

McGregor Campbell, a Detective Sergeant like Rebus, was donning coat and hat.

"What's the word, Mac? Is it going to be a busy night?" Rebus began checking the messages on his desk.

"I don't know about that, John, but I can tell you that it's been pandemonium in here today. There's a letter there for you from the man himself."

"Oh yes?" Rebus seemed preoccupied with another letter which he had just opened.

"Yes, John. Brace yourself. I think you're going to be transferred to that abduction case. Good luck to you. Well, I'm off to the pub. I want to catch the boxing on the BBC. I should be in time." Campbell checked his watch. "Yes, plenty of time. Is anything wrong, John?"

"Who brought this in, Mac?"

"I haven't the faintest, John. What is it?"

"Another crank letter."

"Oh yes?" Campbell sidled over to Rebus's shoulder. He examined the typed note. "Looks like the same bloke, doesn't it?"

"Clever of you to notice that, Mac, seeing as it's the exact same message."

"What about the string?"

"Oh, it's here, too." Rebus lifted a small piece of string from his desk. There was a simple knot tied in its middle.

"Queer bloody business." Campbell walked to the doorway. "See you tomorrow, John."

"Yes, yes, see you, Mac." Rebus paused until his friend had made his exit. "Oh, Mac!" Campbell came back into the doorway.

"Yes?"

"Maxwell won the big fight," said Rebus, smiling.

"God, you're a bastard, Rebus." Gritting his teeth, Campbell stalked out of the station.

"One of the old school," Rebus said to himself. "Now, what possible enemies could I have?"

He studied the letter again, then checked the envelope. It was blank save for his own name, unevenly typed. The note had been handed in, just like the other one. It was a queer bloody business right enough.

He walked back downstairs and headed for the desk.

"Jimmy?"

"Yes, John."

"Have you seen this?" He showed the envelope to the desk sergeant.

"That?" The sergeant wrinkled not only his brow but, it seemed to Rebus, his whole face. Only forty years in the force could do that to a man, forty years of questions and puzzles and crosses to bear. "It must have been put through the door,

John. I found it myself on the floor just there." He pointed vaguely in the direction of the station's front door. "Is anything up?"

"Oh no, it's nothing really. Thanks, Jimmy."

But Rebus knew that he would be niggled all night by the arrival of this note, only days after he had received the first anonymous message. He studied the two letters at his desk. The work of an old typewriter, probably portable. The letter *S* about a millimetre higher than the other letters. The paper cheap, no water-mark. The piece of string, tied in the middle, cut with a sharp knife or scissors. The message. The same typewritten message:

THERE ARE CLUES EVERYWHERE.

Fair enough; perhaps there were. It was the work of a crank, a kind of practical joke. But why him? It made no sense. Then the phone rang.

"Detective Sergeant Rebus?"

"Speaking."

"Rebus, it's Chief Inspector Anderson here. Have you received my note?"

Anderson. Bloody Anderson. That was all he needed. From one crank to another.

"Yes, sir," said Rebus, holding the receiver under his chin and tearing open the letter on his desk.

"Good. Can you be here in twenty minutes? The briefing will be in the Waverley Road Incident Room."

"I'll be there, sir."

The phone went dead on Rebus as he read. It was true then, it was official. He was being transferred to the abduction case. God, what a life. He pushed the messages, envelopes, and string into his jacket pocket, looking around the office in frustration. Who was kidding who? It would take an act of God to get round to finishing all his work? He had three cases coming to court and another dozen or so crying out for some paperwork before his memory of them faded entirely. That would be nice, actually, nice to just erase the lot of them. Wipe-out. He closed his eyes. He opened them again. The paperwork was still there, large as life. Useless. Always incomplete. No sooner had he finished with a case than another two or three appeared in its place. What was the name of that creature? The Hydra, was it? That was what he was fighting. Every time he cut off a head, more popped into his in-tray. Coming back from a holiday was a nightmare.

And now they were giving him rocks to push up hills as well.

He looked to the ceiling.

"With God's grace," he whispered. Then he headed out to his car.

## II

The Sutherland Bar was a popular watering-hole. It contained no jukebox, no video machines, no bandits. The decor was spartan, and the TV usually flickered and jumped. Ladies had not been welcome until well into the 1960s. There had, it seemed, been something to hide: the best pint of draught beer in Edinburgh. McGregor Campbell supped from his heavy glass, his eyes intent on the television set above the bar.

"Who wins?" asked a voice beside him.

"I don't know," he said, turning to the voice. "Oh, hello, Jim."

A stocky man was sitting beside him, money in hand, waiting to be served. His eyes, too, were on the TV.

"Looks like a cracker of a fight," he said. "I fancy Mailer to win."

Mac Campbell had an idea.

"No, I reckon Maxwell will walk it, win by a mile. Fancy a bet?"

The stocky man fished into his pocket for his cigarettes, eyeing the policeman.

"How much?" he asked.

"A fiver?" said Campbell.

"You're on. Tom, give me a pint over here, please. Do you want one yourself, Mac?"

"Same again, thanks."

They sat in silence for a while, supping the beer and watching the fight. A few muffled roars went up occasionally from behind them as a punch landed or was dodged.

"It's looking good for your man if it goes the distance," said Campbell, ordering more drinks.

"Aye. But let's wait and see, eh? How's work, by the way?"

"Fine, how's yours?"

"A pure bloody slog at the moment, if you must ask." Some ash dropped onto his tie as he talked, the cigarette never leaving his mouth, though it wobbled precariously from time to time. "A pure slog."

"Are you still chasing up that drugs story?"

"Not really. I've landed on this kidnapping thing."

"Oh? So has Rebus. You'd better not get into *his* hair."

"Newspapermen get in *everybody's* hair, Mac. It goes with the etcetera."

Mac Campbell, though wary of Jim Stevens, was grateful for a friendship, however tenuous and strained it had sometimes been, which had given him some information useful to his career. Stevens kept much of the juiciest tidbits to himself, of course. That's what "exclusives" were made of. But he was always willing to trade, and it seemed to Campbell that the most innocuous pieces of gossip and information seemed adequate for Stevens's needs. He was a kind of magpie, collecting everything without prejudice, storing much more of it than, surely, he would ever use. But with reporters you never could tell. Certainly, Campbell was happier with Stevens as a friend than as an enemy.

"So what's happening about your drugs dossier?"

Jim Stevens shrugged his creased shoulders.

"There's nothing in there just now that could be of much use to you boys anyway. I'm not about to let the whole thing drop through, if that's what you mean. No, that's too big a nest of vipers to be allowed to go free. I'll still be keeping my eyes open."

A bell rang for the last round of the fight. Two sweating, dog-tired bodies converged on one another, becoming a single knot of limbs.

"Still looks good for Mailer," said Campbell, an uneasy feeling coming over him. It couldn't be true. Rebus wouldn't have done that to him. Suddenly, Maxwell, the heavier and slower-moving of the two fighters, was hit by a blow to the face and staggered back. The bar erupted, sensing blood and victory. Campbell stared into his glass. Maxwell was taking a standing count. It was all over. A sensation in the final seconds of the contest, according to the commentator.

Jim Stevens held out his hand.

I'll kill bloody Rebus, thought Campbell. So help me, I'll kill him.

Later, over drinks bought with Campbell's money, Jim Stevens asked about Rebus.

"So it looks as if I'll be meeting him at last?"

"Maybe, maybe not. He's not exactly friendly with Anderson, so he may well get the shitty end of the stick, sitting at a desk all day. But then John Rebus isn't exactly friendly with anybody."

"Oh?"

"Ach, he's not that bad, I suppose, but he's not the easiest of men to like." Campbell, ducking from his friend's interrogative eyes, studied the reporter's tie. The recent layer of cigarette-ash had merely formed a veil over much older stains. Egg, perhaps, fat, alcohol. The scruffiest reporters were always the sharp ones, and Stevens was sharp, as sharp as ten years on the local newspaper could make a man. It was said that he had turned down jobs with London papers, just because he liked to live in Edinburgh. And what he liked best about his job was the opportunity it gave him to uncover the city's murkier depths, the crime, the corruption, the gangs, and the drugs. He was a better detective than anyone Campbell knew, and, because of that very fact perhaps, the high-ups in the police both disliked and distrusted him. That seemed proof enough that he was doing his job well. Campbell watched as a little beer escaped from Stevens's glass and dripped onto his trousers.

"This Rebus," said Stevens, wiping his mouth, "he's the brother of the hypnotist, isn't he?"

"Must be. I've never asked him, but there can't be too many people about with a name like that, can there?"

"That's what I was thinking." He nodded to himself as though confirming something of great importance.

"So what?"

"Oh, nothing. Just something. And he's not a popular man, you say?"

"I didn't say that exactly. I feel sorry for him really. The poor bugger has a lot on his plate. He's even started getting crank letters."

"Crank letters?" Smoke enveloped Stevens for a moment as he puffed on another cigarette. Between the two men lay a thin blue pub-haze.

"I shouldn't have told you that. That was *strictly* off the record."

Stevens nodded.

"Absolutely. No, it's just that I was interested. That sort of thing does happen though, doesn't it?"

"Not often. And not nearly as queer as the ones he's getting. I mean, they're not abusive or anything. They're just . . . queer."

"Go on. How so?"

"Well, there's a bit of string in each one, tied into a knot, and there's a message that reads something like 'clues are everywhere.' "

"Bloody hell. That is strange. They're a strange family. One a bloody hypnotist and the other getting anonymous notes. He was in the Army, wasn't he?"

"John was, yes. How did you know?"

"I know everything, Mac. That's the job."

"Another funny thing is that he won't speak about it."

The reporter looked interested again. When he was interested in something, his shoulders shivered slightly. He stared at the television.

"Won't speak about the army?"

"Not a word. I've asked him about it a couple of times."

"Like I said, Mac, it's a funny family, that one. Drink up, I've got lots of your money left to spend."

"You're a bastard, Jim."

"Born and bred," said the reporter, smiling for only the second time that evening.

## III

"Gentlemen, and, of course, ladies, thank you for being so quick to gather here. This will remain the centre of operations during the inquiry. Now, as you all know . . ."

Detective Chief Superintendent Wallace froze in mid-speech as the Inquiry Room door pushed itself open abruptly and John Rebus, all eyes turned towards him, entered the room. He looked about in embarrassment, smiled a hopeful but wasted apology towards the senior officer, and sat himself down on a chair nearest to the door.

"As I was saying," continued the superintendent.

Rebus, rubbing at his forehead, studied the roomful of officers. He knew what the old boy would be saying, and right now the last thing he needed was a pep-talk of the old school. The room was packed. Many of them looked tired, as if they'd been on the case for a while. The fresher, more attentive faces belonged to the new boys, some of them brought in from stations outwith the city. Two or three had notebooks and pencils at the ready, almost as if they were back in the school classroom. And at the front of the group, legs crossed, sat two women, peering up at Wallace, who was in full flight now, parading before the blackboard like some Shakespearean hero in a bad school play.

"Two deaths, then. Yes, deaths I'm afraid." The room shivered expectantly. "The body of Sandra Adams, aged eleven, was found on a piece of waste ground adjacent to Haymarket Station at six o'clock this evening, and that of Mary Andrews at six-fifty on an allotment in the Oxgrange district. There are officers at both locations, and at the end of this briefing more of you will be selected to join them."

Rebus was noticing that the usual pecking-order was in play: inspectors near the front of the room, D.S.s and the rest to the back. Even in the midst of murder, there is a pecking-order. The British Disease. And he was at the bottom of the pile, because he had arrived late. Another black mark against him on someone's mental sheet.

He had always been one of the top men while he had been in the Army. He had been a Para. He had trained for the SAS and come out top of his class. He had been chosen for a crack Special Assignments group. He had his medal and his commendations. It had been a good time, and yet it had been the worst of times, too, a time of stress and deprivation, of deceit and brutality. And when he had left, the police had been reluctant to take him. He understood now that it was something to do with the pressure applied by the Army to get him the job that he wanted. Some people resented that, and they had thrown down banana skins ever since for him to slide on. But he had side-stepped their traps, had performed the job, and had grudgingly been given his commendations here also. But there was precious little promotion, and that had caused him to say a few things out of line, a few things that were always to be held against him. And then he had cuffed an unruly bastard one night in the cells. God forgive him, he had simply lost his head for a minute. There had been more trouble over that. Ah, but it was not a nice world this, not a nice world at all. It was an Old Testament land that he found himself in, a land of barbarity and retribution.

"We will, of course, have more information for you to work on come tomorrow, after the post-mortems. But for the moment I think that will do. I'm going to hand you over to Chief

Inspector Anderson, who will assign you to your tasks for the present."

Rebus noticed that Jack Morton had nodded off in the corner and, if left unattended, would begin snoring soon. Rebus smiled, but the smile was short-lived, killed by a voice at the front of the room, the voice of Anderson. This was all Rebus needed. Anderson, the man at the centre of his out-of-line remarks. It felt for one sickening moment like predestination. Anderson was in charge. Anderson was doling out their tasks. Rebus reminded himself to stop praying. Perhaps if he stopped prayer, God would take the hint and stop being such a bastard to one of his few believers on this near-godforsaken planet.

"Gemmill and Hartley will be assigned to door-to-door."

Well, thank God he'd not been landed with that one. There was only one thing worse than door-to-door . . .

"And for an initial check on the M.O. files, Detective Sergeants Morton and Rebus."

*Thank you, God, oh, thank you. That's just what I wanted to do with my evening: read through the case histories of all the bloody perverts and sex-offenders in east central Scotland. You must really hate my guts. Am I Job or something? Is that it?*

But there was no ethereal voice to be heard, no voice at all save that of the satanic, leering Anderson, whose fingers slowly turned the pages of the roster, his lips moist and full, his wife a known adulteress and his son—of all things—an itinerant poet. Rebus heaped curse after curse upon the shoulders of that priggish, stick-thin superior officer, then kicked Jack Morton's leg and brought him snorting and chaffing into consciousness.

One of those nights.

## IV

"One of those nights," said Jack Morton. He sucked luxuriously on his short, tipped cigarette, coughed loudly, brought his handkerchief from his pocket and deposited something into it from his mouth. He studied the contents of the handkerchief. "Ah ha, some vital new evidence," he said. All the same, he looked rather worried.

Rebus smiled. "Time to stop smoking, Jack," he said.

They were seated together at a desk upon which were piled about a hundred and fifty files on known sex-offenders in central Scotland. A smart young secretary, doubtless relishing the overtime that came with a murder inquiry, kept bringing more files into the office, and Rebus stared at her in mock outrage every time she entered. He was hoping to scare her away, and if she came back again, the outrage would become real.

"No, John, it's these tipped bastards. I can't take them, really I can't. Sod that bloody doctor."

So saying, Morton took the cigarette from his lips, broke off the filter, and replaced the cigarette, now ridiculously short, between thin, bloodless lips.

"That better. That's more like a fag."

Rebus had always found two things remarkable. One was that he liked, and in return was liked by, Jack Morton. The other was that Morton could pull so hard on a cigarette and yet release so little smoke. Where did all that smoke go? He could not figure it out.

"I see you're abstaining this evening, John."

"Limiting myself to ten a day, Jack."

Morton shook his head.

"Ten, twenty, thirty a day. Take it from me, John, it makes no difference in the end. What it comes down to is this: you either stop or you don't, and if you can't stop, then you're as well smoking as many as you like. That's been proven. I read about it in a magazine."

"Aye, but we all know the magazines *you* read, Jack."

Morton chuckled, gave another tremendous cough, and searched for his handkerchief.

"What a bloody job," said Rebus, picking up the first of the files.

The two men sat in silence for twenty minutes, flicking through the facts and fantasies of rapists, exhibitionists, pederasts, paedophiles, and procurers. Rebus felt his mouth filling with silt. It was as if he saw himself there, time after time after time, the self that lurked behind his everyday consciousness. His Mister Hyde by Robert Louis Stevenson, Edinburgh-born. He felt ashamed of his occasional erection: doubtless Jack Morton had one, too. It came with the territory, as did the revulsion, the loathing, and the fascination.

Around them, the station whirled in the business of the night. Men in shirtsleeves walked purposefully past their open door, the door of their assigned office, cut off from everyone else so that no one would be contaminated by their thoughts. Rebus paused for a moment to reflect that his own office back in Great London Road was in need of much of this equipment: the modern desk (unwobbly, with drawers that could be opened easily), the filing-cabinets (ditto), the drinks-dispenser just outside. There were carpets even, rather than his own liver-red linoleum with its curled, dangerous edges. It was a very palatable environment this in which to track down the odd pervert or killer.

"What exactly are we looking for, Jack?"

Morton snorted, threw down a slender brown file, looked at Rebus, shrugged his shoulders, and lit a cigarette.

"Garbage," he said, picking up another folder, and whether or not it was meant as an answer Rebus was never to know.

"Detective Sergeant Rebus?"

A young constable, ance on his throat, cleanly-shaven, stood at the open door.

"Yes."

"Message from the Chief, sir."

He handed Rebus a folded piece of blue notepaper.

"Good news?" asked Morton.

"Oh, the best news, Jack, the very best news. Our boss sends us the following fraternal message: 'Any leads from the files?' End of message."

"Will there be any reply, sir?" asked the constable.

Rebus crumpled the note and tossed it into a new aluminium bin.

"Yes, son, there will be," he said, "but I very much doubt whether you'd want to deliver it."

Jack Morton, wiping ash from his tie, laughed.

It was one of those nights. Jim Stevens, walking home at long last, had not found anything interesting since his conversation with Mac Campbell all of four hours ago. He had told Mac then that he was not about to drop his own investigation into Edinburgh's burgeoning drugs racket, and that had been the whole truth. It was becoming a private obsession, and though his boss might move him on to a murder case, still he would follow up his old investigation in his free, spare, and private time, time found late at night when the presses were rolling, time spent in lower and lower dives further and further out of town. For he was close, he knew, to a big fish, and yet not close enough to be able to enlist the help of the forces of law. He wanted the story to be watertight before he called for the cavalry.

He knew the dangers, too. The ground he walked upon was always likely to fall away beneath his feet, letting him slip into Leith docks of a dark and silent morning, finding him trussed and gagged in some motorway ditch outside Perth. He didn't mind all that. It was no more than a passing thought, brought on by tiredness and a need to lift his emotions out of the rather tawdry, unglamorous world of Edinburgh's dope scene, a scene carried out in the sprawling housing-schemes and after-hours drinking holes more than in the glittery discotheques and chintzy rooms of the New Town.

What he disliked, really disliked, was that the people ultimately behind it all were so silent and so secretive and so alien
to it all. He liked his criminals to be involved, to live the life
and stick close to the lifestyle. He liked the Glasgow gangster
of the 1950s and '60s, who lived in the Gorbals and operated
from the Gorbals and loaned illicit money to neighbours, and
who would slash those same neighbours eventually, when the
need arose. It was like a family affair. Not like this, not at all
like this. This was other, and he hated it for that reason.

His talk with Campbell had been interesting though, interesting for other reasons. Rebus sounded a fishy character. So
was his brother. They might be in it together. If the police
were involved in all of this, then his task would be all the
harder, and all the more satisfying for that.

Now what he needed was a break, a nice break in the
investigation. It couldn't be far off. He was supposed to have a
nose for that sort of thing.

## V

At one-thirty they took a break. There was a small canteen in
the building, open even at this ungodly hour. Outside, the
majority of the day's petty crime was being committed, but
inside it was warm and cosy, and there was hot food to be had
and endless cups of coffee for the vigilant policemen.

"This is a sodding shambles," said Morton, pouring coffee
back from his saucer into the cup. "Anderson hasn't a clue
what he's up to."

"Give me a cigarette, will you? I'm out." Rebus patted his
pockets convincingly.

"Christ, John," said Morton, wheezing an old man's cough
and passing across the cigarettes, "the day you give up smoking is the day I change my underwear."

Jack Morton was not an old man, despite the excesses that
were leading him quickly and inexorably towards that early
fate. He was thirty-five, six years younger than Rebus. He, too,

had a broken marriage behind him, the four children now resident with their grandmother while their mother was off on a suspiciously long vacation with her present lover. Misery, he had told Rebus, surrounded the whole bloody set-up, and Rebus had agreed with him, having a daughter who troubled his own conscious.

Morton had been a policeman for two decades, and unlike Rebus had started at the extreme bottom of the heap, pulling himself up to his present rank through sheer hard slog alone. He had given Rebus his life story when the two of them had gone off for a day's fly-fishing near Berwick. It had been a glorious day, both of them landing fine catches, and over the course of the day they had become friends. Rebus, however, had not deigned to tell his own life story to Morton. It felt, to Jack Morton, as if the man were in a little prison-cell of his own construction. He seemed especially tight-lipped about his years in the Army. Morton knew that the Army could occasionally do that to a man, and he respected Rebus's silence. Perhaps there were a few skeletons in that particular closet. He knew all about those himself; some of his most noteworthy arrests had not exactly been conducted along "correct procedural lines."

Nowadays, Morton did not concern himself with headlines and high-profile arrests. He got on with his job, collected his salary, thought now and then of his pension and the fishing-years to come, and drank his wife and children out of his conscience.

"This is a nice canteen," said Rebus, smoking, struggling to start a conversation.

"Yes, it is. I'm in here now and again. I know one of the guys who work in the computer room. Comes in handy, you know, having one of those terminal-operators in your pocket. They can track down a car, a name, an address quicker than you can blink. It only costs the occasional drink."

"Get them to sort out this lot of ours then."

"Give them time, John. Then *all* the files will be on computer. And a little while after that, they'll find that they don't

need the work-horses like us any more. There'll just be a
couple of D.I.s and a desk console."

"I'll bear that in mind," said Rebus.

"It's progress, John. Where would we be without it? We'd
still be out there with our pipes and our guess-work and our
magnifying glasses."

"I suppose you're right, Jack. But remember what the
Super says: 'Give me a dozen good men every time, and send
your machines back to their makers.'"

Rebus looked around him as he spoke. He saw that one of
the two women from the briefing room had settled at a table
by herself.

"And besides," said Rebus, "there'll always be a place for
people like us, Jack. Society couldn't do without us. Com-
puters can never have inspired guesses. That's where we've
got them beat hands down."

"Maybe, I don't know. Still, we better be getting back, eh?"
Morton looked at his watch, drained his cup, and pushed back
his chair.

"You go on ahead, Jack. I'll be with you in a minute. I want
to check out an inspired guess."

"Mind if I join you?"

Rebus, a fresh cup of coffee in his hand, pulled out the chair
from opposite the woman officer, who had her head buried in
the day's newspaper. He noted the garish headline on the
front page. Someone had slipped out a little information to
the local media.

"Not at all," she said, not looking up.

Rebus smiled to himself and sat down. He began to sip the
powdery, instant murk.

"Busy?" he asked.

"Yes. Shouldn't you be? Your friend left a few minutes ago."

Sharp then, very sharp. Very, very sharp indeed. Rebus
began to feel a mite uneasy. He disliked ballcrushers, and
here were all the outward signs of one.

"Yes, he did, didn't he? But then he's a glutton for punishment. We're working on the Modus Operandi files. I'd do anything to defer that particular pleasure."

She looked up at last, bitten by the potential insult.

"That's what I am, is it? A delaying tactic?"

Rebus smiled and shrugged.

"What else?" he said.

It was her turn to smile now. She closed the paper and folded it twice, placing it before her on the formica-topped table. She tapped the headline.

"Looks like we're in the news," she said.

Rebus turned the paper towards him.

EDINBURGH ABDUCTIONS—NOW IT'S MURDER!

"A terrible bloody case," he offered. "Just terrible. And the newspapers don't make it any better."

"Yes, well, we'll have the P.M. results in a couple of hours, and then we just might have something to go on."

"I hope so. Just so long as I can put away those bloody files."

"I thought policemen," stressing the latter part of the word, "got their kicks from reading that stuff."

Rebus spread his hands before him, a gesture he seemed to have picked up from Michael.

"You have us to a *T.* How long have you been in the force?"

Rebus took her to be thirty, give or take two years. She had thick, short brown hair, and a long, straight ski-slope of a nose. There were no rings on her fingers, but these days that told him nothing.

"Long enough," she said.

"I think I knew you would say that."

She was smiling still: no ballcrusher then.

"Then you're cleverer than I took you for," she said.

"You'd be surprised."

He was growing tired, realising that the game was going nowhere. It was all midfield, a friendly rather than a cup-tie. He checked his watch conspicuously.

"Time I was getting back," he said.

She picked up her newspaper.

"Are you doing anything this weekend?" she asked.

John Rebus sat down again.

## VI

He left the station at four o'clock. The birds were doing their best to persuade everyone that it was dawn, but no one seemed fooled. It was dark still, and the air was chilled.

He decided to leave his car and walk home, a distance of two miles. He needed it, needed to feel the cool, damp air, the expectancy of a morning shower. He breathed deep, trying to relax, to forget, but his mind was too full of those files, and little pieces of recollected fact and figure, pieces of horror no bigger than a paragraph, haunted his walk.

To indecently assault an eight-week-old baby girl. The babysitter who had calmly admitted to the assault saying that she had done it "for a kick."

To rape a grandmother in front of her two grandchildren, then give the kids some sweets from a jar before leaving. The act premeditated; committed by a bachelor of fifty.

To burn with cigarettes the name of a street gang onto the breasts of a twelve-year-old, leaving her for dead in a burning hut. Never caught.

And now the crux: to abduct two girls and then strangle them *without* having sexually abused them. That, Anderson had posited only thirty minutes before, was a perversion in itself, and in a funny way Rebus knew what he meant. It made the deaths even more arbitrary, more pointless—and more shocking.

Well, at least they were not dealing with a sex-offender; not right away. Which only, Rebus was forced to agree, made their task that much more difficult, for now they were confronted with something like a "serial killer," striking at random and without clues, aiming at the record books rather than at any idea of "kicks." The question now was would he stop at two? It seemed unlikely.

Strangulation. It was a fearful way to go, wrestling, kicking your way towards oblivion, panic, the fretful sucking for air, and the killer behind you most likely, so that you faced the fear of something totally anonymous, a death without knowledge of who or why. Rebus had been taught methods of killing in the SAS. He knew what it felt like to have the garotte tighten on your neck, trusting to the opponent's prevailing sanity. A fearful way to go.

Edinburgh slept on, as it had slept on for hundreds of years. There were ghosts in the cobbled alleys and on the twisting stairways of the Old Town tenements, but they were Enlightenment ghosts, articulate and deferential. They were not about to leap from the darkness with a length of twine ready in their hands. Rebus paused and looked around him. Besides, it was morning now and any godfearing spirit would be tucked up in bed, as he, John Rebus, flesh and blood, would be soon.

Near his flat, he passed a little grocery shop outside of which were stacked crates of milk and morning rolls. The owner had complained in private to Rebus about petty and occasional thefts, but would not submit a complaint proper. The shop was as dead as the street, the solitude of the moment disturbed only by the distant rumble of a taxi on cobblestones and the persistence of the dawn chorus. Rebus looked around him, examining the many curtained windows. Then, swiftly, he tore six rolls from a layer and stuffed them into his pockets, walking away a little too briskly. A moment later he hesitated, then walked on tiptoe back to the shop, the criminal returning to the scene of the crime, the dog to its vomit. Rebus had never actually seen dogs doing that, but he had it on the authority of Saint Peter.

Looking round again, he lifted a pint of milk out of its crate and made his getaway, whistling silently to himself.

Nothing in the world tasted as good for breakfast as stolen

rolls with some butter and jam and a mug of milky coffee. Nothing tasted better than a venial sin.

He sniffed t᠌ ᴐ stairwell of his tenement, catching the faint odour of tom-cats, a persistent menace. He held his breath as he climbed the two flights of stairs, fumbling in his pocket beneath the squashed rolls, trying to liberate his door-key.

The interior of the flat felt damp and smelt damp. He checked the central heating and, sure enough, the pilot-light had gone out again. He cursed as he relit it, turning the heat up all the way, and went through to the living-room.

There were still spaces on the bookcase, the wall-unit, the mantelpiece where Rhona's ornaments had once stood, but many of the gaps had already been filled by new mementoes of his own: bills, unanswered letters, old ring-pulls from tins of cheap beer, the occasional unread book. Rebus collected unread books. Once upon a time, he had actually read the books that he bought, but these days he seemed to have so little time. Also, he was more discriminating now than he had been then, back in the old days when he would read a book to its bitter end whether he liked it or not. These days, a book he disliked was unlikely to last ten pages of his concentration.

These were the books that lay around his living-room. His books for reading tended to congregate in the bedroom, lying in co-ordinated rows on the floor like patients in a doctor's waiting-room. One of these days he would take a holiday, would rent a cottage in the Highlands or on the Fife coast, and would take with him all of these waiting-to-be-read-or-reread books, all of that knowledge that could be his for the breaking open of a cover. His favourite book, a book he turned to at least once a year, was *Crime and Punishment.* If only, he thought, modern murderers would exhibit some show of conscience more often. But no, modern killers bragged of their crimes to their friends, then played pool in their local pub, chalking their cues with poise and certainty, knowing which balls would drop in which order . . .

While a police car slept nearby, its occupants unable to do anything save curse the mountains of rules and regulations and rue the deep chasms of crime. It was everywhere, crime. It was the life-force and the blood and the balls of life: to cheat, to edge, to take that body-swerve at authority, to kill. The higher up you climbed into crime, the more subtly you began to move back towards legitimacy, until a handful of lawyers only could crack open your system, and they were always affordable, always on hand to be bribed. Dostoevsky had known all that, clever old bastard. He had felt the stick burning from both ends.

But poor old Dostoevsky was dead and had not been invited to a party this weekend, while he, John Rebus, had. Often he declined invitations, because to accept meant that he had to dust off his brogues, iron a shirt, brush down his best suit, take a bath, and splash on some cologne. He had also to be affable, to drink and be merry, to talk to strangers with whom he had no inclination to talk and with whom he was not being paid to talk. In other words, he resented having to play the part of a normal human animal. But he had accepted the invitation given to him by Cathy Jackson in the Waverley Road canteen.

And he whistled at the thought of it, wandering through to the kitchen to make some breakfast, which he then took through to his bedroom. This was a ritual after a night duty. He stripped, climbed into bed, balanced the plate of rolls on his chest, and held a book to his nose. It was not a very good book. It was about a kidnapping. Rhona had taken away the bed proper, but had left him the mattress, so it was easy for him to reach down for his mug of coffee, easy for him to discard one book and find another.

He fell asleep soon enough, the lamp still burning, as cars began to pass by his window.

His alarm did the trick for a change, pulling him off the mattress as a magnet attracts filings. He had kicked off the duvet, and was drenched in sweat. He felt suffocated, and remembered suddenly that the central heating was still boiling away like a steamship. On his way to switching off the thermostat, he stooped at the front door to pick up the day's mail. One of the letters was unstamped and unfranked. It bore only his name in typescript across the front. Rebus's stomach squeezed hard on the paste of rolls and butter. He ripped the envelope open, pulling out the single sheet of paper.

FOR THOSE WHO READ BETWEEN THE TIMES.

So now the bastard knew where he stayed. Checking in the envelope, laconic now and expecting to find the knotted string, he found instead two matchsticks, tied together with thread into the shape of a cross.

# PART TWO

## *"For Those Who Read*
## *Between the Times"*

### VII

Organized chaos: that summed up the newspaper office. Organized chaos on the grandest of scales. Stevens rummaged amongst the sheaf of paper in his tray, looking for a needle. Had he perhaps filed it somewhere else? He opened one of the large, heavy drawers of his desk, then shut it quickly, afraid that some of the mess in there might escape. Controlling himself, he took a deep breath and opened it again. He plunged a hand into the jumble of paper inside the drawer, as if something in there would bite. A huge dog-clip, springing loose from one particular file, did bite. It nicked his thumb and he slammed the drawer shut, the cigarette wobbling in his mouth as he cursed the office, the journalistic profession, and trees, begetters of paper. Sod it. He sat back and squeezed his eyes shut as the smoke began to sting. It was eleven in the morning, and already the office was a blue haze, as though everything were happening on the set of a *Brigadoon* marsh-scene. He grabbed a sheet of typescript, turned it over, and began to scribble with a nub of pencil which he had lifted from a betting shop.

"X (Mr Big?) delivers to Rebus, M. How does the policeman fit in? Answer—perhaps everywhere, perhaps nowhere."

He paused, taking the cigarette from his mouth, replacing it with a fresh one, and using the butt to light its successor.

"Now—anonymous letters. Threats? A code?"

Stevens found it unlikely that John Rebus could not know about his brother's involvement in the Scottish drug-pushing world, and knowing, the chances were that he was involved in it, too, perhaps leading the whole investigation the wrong way to protect his flesh and blood. It would make a cracking good story when it broke, but he knew that he would be treading on eggs from here on in. No one would go out of their way to help him nail a policeman, and if anyone found out what he was up to, he would be in very serious trouble indeed. He needed to do two things: check his life insurance policy, and tell nobody about this.

"Jim!"

The editor gestured for him to step into the torture chamber. He rose from his seat, as though tearing himself up from something organic, straightened his mauve-and-pink striped tie, and headed towards a presumed bawling-out.

"Yes, Tom?"

"Aren't you supposed to be at a press conference?"

"Plenty of time, Tom."

"Which photographer are you taking?"

"Does it matter? I'd be better off taking my bloody instamatic. These young boys don't know the ropes, Tom. What about Andy Fleming? Can't I have him?"

"No chance, Jim. He's covering the royal tour."

"What royal tour?"

Tom Jameson seemed about to rise again from his chair, which would have been an unprecedented move. He only straightened his back and shoulders however, and eyed his "star" crime reporter suspiciously.

"You *are* a journalist, Jim, aren't you? I mean, you've not gone into early retirement, or become a recluse? No history of senile dementia in the family?"

"Listen, Tom, when the Royal Family commits a crime, I'll be the first on the scene. Otherwise, as far as I'm concerned, they don't exist. Not outside of my nightmares, anyway."

Jameson pointedly examined his wristwatch.

"Okay, okay, I'm going."

With that, Stevens turned on his heels with amazing speed and left the office, ignoring the cries of his boss at his back, asking which of the available photographers he wanted.

It wouldn't matter. He had yet to meet a policeman who was photogenic. Then, leaving the building, he remembered who was Liaison Officer on this particular case, and he changed his mind, smiling.

" 'There are clues everywhere, for those who read between the times.' It's pure gobbledygook, isn't it, John?"

Morton was driving the car towards the Haymarket district of the city. It was another afternoon of consistent, wind-driven rain, the rain itself fine and cold, the kind that seeped into bones and marrow. The city had been dull all day, to a point where motorists were using their headlamps at noon. A great day for some outside work.

"I'm not so sure, Jack. The second part leads on from the first as if there was a logical connection."

"Well, let's hope he sends you some more notes. Maybe that would make things clearer."

"Maybe. I'd rather he'd just stop this shit altogether. It's not very nice knowing that a crank knows where you work and where you live."

"Is your phone number in the telephone book?"

"No, unlisted."

"That rules out that idea then. So how does he know your home address?"

"He *or* she," said Rebus, tucking the notes back into his pocket. "How should I know?"

He lit two cigarettes and passed one to Morton, breaking the filter off for him.

"Ta," said Morton, placing the tiny cigarette in the corner of his mouth. The rain was easing. "Floods in Glasgow," he said, expecting no reply.

Both men were bleary-eyed from lack of sleep, but the case had taken possession of them, so they drove, minds numbed, towards the bleak heart of the inquiry. A portakabin had been set up on the waste ground next to the spot where the girl's body had been found. From there, a door-to-door operation was being co-ordinated. Friends and family were also to be interviewed. Rebus foresaw much tedium in the day ahead.

"What worries me," Morton had said, "is that if the two murders are linked, then we're dealing with someone who probably didn't know either of the girls. *That* makes for a bastard of a job."

Rebus had nodded. There was still the chance, however, either that both girls had known their murderer, or that the murderer had been someone in a position of trust. Otherwise, the girls being nearly twelve years old and not daft, they would surely have struggled when abducted. Yet no one had come forward to say that they had witnessed any such thing. It was bloody strange.

The rain had stopped by the time they reached the cramped operations-room. The inspector in charge of out-door operations was there to hand them lists of names and addresses. Rebus rejoiced to be away from the HQ, away from Anderson and his thirst for paperwork results. *This* was where the work really took place, where the contacts were made, where one slip by a suspect could tip a case one way or the other.

"Do you mind me asking, sir, who it was that suggested my colleague and me for this particular job?"

The D.I., his eyes twinkling, studied Rebus for a second.

"Yes, I bloody well do mind, Rebus. It doesn't matter one way or the other, does it? Every single task in this case is as vital and as important as every other. Let's not forget that."

"Yes, sir," said Rebus.

"This must be a bit like working inside a shoebox, sir," said Morton, examining the cramped interior.

"Yes, son, I'm in the shoebox, but you lot are the shoes, so get bloody well moving."

This particular inspector, thought Rebus, pocketing his list, seemed a nice bloke, his tongue just sharp enough for Rebus's taste.

"Don't worry, sir," he said now, "this won't take us long."

He hoped that the inspector noted the irony in his voice.

"Last one back's a fairy," said Morton.

They were doing this by the rule-book then, yet the case would seem to demand that new rules be drawn up. Anderson was sending them out to look for the usual suspects: family, acquaintances, people with records. Doubtless, back at HQ, groups such as the Paedophile Information Exchange were being investigated. Rebus hoped that there were plenty of crank calls for Anderson to sift through. There usually were: the callers who admitted to the crime, the callers who were psychic and could help by getting in touch with the deceased, the callers who pressed a red-herring to your nose so that you could have a sniff. They were all mastered by past guilt and present fantasies. Perhaps everyone was.

At his first house, Rebus battered on the door and waited. It was opened by a rank old woman, her feet bare, a cardigan comprised of ninety-percent hole to ten-percent wool hanging around her scarp-like shoulders.

"Whit is it?"

"Police, madam. It's about the murder."

"Eh? Whitever it is, I dinnae want it. Away ye get afore I ca' for the coppers."

"The murders," shouted Rebus. "I'm a policeman. I've come to ask you a few questions."

"Eh?" She stood back a little to peer at him, and Rebus could swear that he saw the faint glow of a past intelligence in the dulled black of her pupils.

"Whit murders?" she said.

One of these days. To improve matters, the rain began again, heavy dollops of stinging water gripping to his neck and face, seeping into his shoes. Just like that day at the old man's grave . . . Only yesterday? A lot could happen in twenty-four hours, all of it to him.

By seven o'clock, Rebus had covered six of the fourteen individuals on his list. He walked back to the operations-shoebox, his feet sore, his stomach awash with tea and craving something stronger.

At the boggy waste ground, Jack Morton stood and stared out over the acres of clay, strewn with bricks and detritus: a child's heaven.

"What a hellish place to die in."

"She didn't die here, Jack. Remember what forensic said."

"Well, you know what I mean."

Yes, Rebus knew what he meant.

"By the way," said Morton, "you're the fairy."

"I'll drink to that," said Rebus.

They drank in some of Edinburgh's seedier bars, bars the tourist never sees. They tried to shut the case out of their minds, but could not. It was like that with big murder inquiries; they got to you, physically and mentally, consuming you and making you work all the harder. There was a rush of pure adrenalin behind every murder. It kept them going past the point of no return.

"I'd better be getting back to the flat," said Rebus.

"No, have another."

Jack Morton weaved towards the bar, his empty glass in his hand.

Rebus, his mind foggy, thought more about his mysterious correspondent. He suspected Rhona, though it could not be said to be her style. He suspected his daughter Sammy, perhaps taking a delayed-action revenge for her father's dismissal of her from his life. Family and acquaintances were, initially at least, always the chief suspects. But it could be anyone, anyone who knew where he worked and where he lived. Someone in his own force was always a possibility to be feared.

The 10,000 dollar question, as ever, was why?

"Here we go, two lovely pints of beer, *gratis* from the management."

"I call that very public-spirited," said Rebus.

"Or publican-spirited, eh, John?" Morton chuckled at his joke, wiping froth from his top lip. He noticed that Rebus wasn't laughing. "A penny for them," he said.

"A serial killer," said Rebus. "It must be. In which case we've not seen the last of our friend's handiwork."

Morton put down his glass, suddenly not very thirsty.

"Those girls went to different schools," continued Rebus, "lived in different areas of the city, had different tastes, different friends, were of different religions, and were killed by the same murderer in the same way and without noticeable abuse of any kind. We're dealing with a maniac. He could be anywhere."

A fight was breaking out at the bar, apparently over a game of dominoes which had gone very badly wrong. A glass fell to the floor, followed by a hush in the bar. Then everyone seemed to calm down a little. One man was led outside by his supporters in the argument. Another remained slumped against the bar, muttering to a woman beside him.

Morton took a gulp of beer.

"Thank God we're off duty," he said. Then: "Fancy a curry?"

Morton finished the chicken vindaloo and threw his fork down on to the plate.

"I reckon I ought to have a word with the Health Department boys," he said, still chewing. "Either that or the Trading Standards. Whatever that was, it wasn't chicken."

They were in a small curry-house near Haymarket Station. Purple lighting, red flock wallpaper, a churning wall of sitar music.

"You looked as if you were enjoying it," said Rebus, finishing his beer.

"Oh yes, I enjoyed it, but it wasn't chicken."

"Well, there's nothing to complain about if you enjoyed it."

Rebus sat slant-wise on his chair, his legs straight out before him, an arm along the chair's back while he smoked his umpteenth cigarette that day.

Morton leaned unsteadily towards his partner.

"John, there's *always* something to complain about, especially if you think you can get off with not paying the bill by doing so."

He winked at Rebus, sat back, burped, and reached into his pocket for a cigarette.

"Garbage," he said.

Rebus tried to count the number of cigarettes he himself had smoked that day, but his brain told him that such calculations were not to be attempted.

"I wonder what our friend the murderer is up to at this exact moment?" he said.

"Finishing a curry?" suggested Morton. "Trouble is, John, he could be one of these Joe Normal types, clean on the surface, married with kids, your average suburban hardworking chap, but underneath a nutter, pure and simple."

"There's nothing simple about our man."

"True."

"But you could well be right. You mean that he's a sort of Jekyll and Hyde, right?"

"Exactly." Morton flicked ash onto the table-top, already splashed with curry sauce and beer. He was peering at his empty plate as though wondering where all the food had gone. "Jekyll and Hyde. You've got it in a nutshell. I'll tell you, John, I'd lock these bastards up for a million years, a million years of solitary in a cell the size of a shoebox. That's what I'd do."

Rebus was staring at the flock wallpaper. He thought back to his own days in solitary, days when the SAS were trying to crack him, days of the ultimate testing, of sighs and of silence, starvation and filth. No, he wouldn't want that again. And yet they had not beaten him, not really beaten him. The others had not been so lucky.

*Trapped in its cell, the face screaming*
*Let me out Let me out*

*Let me out . . .*

"John? Are you okay there? If you're going to be sick, the toilet's behind the kitchen. Listen, when you're passing, do me a favour and see if you can notice what it is that they're chopping up and throwing into the pot . . ."

Rebus walked smartly to the toilet with the over-cautious gait of the tremendously drunk, yet he did not feel drunk, not *that* drunk. His nostrils filled with the smells of curry, disinfectant, shit. He washed his face. No, he was not going to be sick. It wasn't too much to drink, for he had felt the same shudder at Michael's, the same momentary horror. What was happening to him? It was as if his insides were concretizing, slowing him down, allowing the years to catch up on him. It felt a little like the nervous breakdown which he had been awaiting, yet it was no nervous breakdown. It was nothing. It had passed.

"Can I give you a lift, John?"

"No thanks, I'll walk. Clear my head."

They parted at the door of the restaurant. An office-party, loosened neckties and strong, sickly perfume, made its way towards Haymarket Station. Haymarket was the last station into Edinburgh before the much grander Waverley Station. Rebus remembered that the premature withdrawal of the penis during intercourse for contraceptive reasons was often referred to as "getting off at Haymarket." Who said that the people in Edinburgh were dour? A smile, a song, and a strangulation. Rebus wiped sweat from his forehead. He felt weak still, and leaned against a lamp-post. He knew vaguely what it was. It was a rejection by his whole being of the past, as though his vital organs were rejecting a donor heart. He had pushed the horror of the training so far to the back of his mind that any echo of it at all was now to be violently fought against. And yet it was in that same confinement that he had found friendship, brotherhood, camaraderie, call it what you like. And he had learned more about himself than human beings ever do. He had learned so much.

His spirit had not been broken. He had come out of the
training on top. And then had come the nervous breakdown.

Enough. He began to walk, steadying himself with thoughts
of his day off tomorrow. He would spend the day reading and
sleeping and readying himself for a party, Cathy Jackson's
party.

And the day after that, Sunday, he would be spending a rare
day with his daughter. Then, perhaps, he would find out who
was behind the crank letters.


## VIII

The girl woke up with a dry, salty taste in her mouth. She felt
sleepy and numb and wondered where she was. She had
fallen asleep in his car. She had not felt sleepy before then,
before he had given her a piece of his chocolate-bar. Now she
was awake, but not in her bedroom at home. This room had
pictures on its walls, pictures cut out of colour magazines.
Some were photographs of soldiers with fierce expressions on
their faces, others were of girls and women. She looked
closely at some self-developing photographs grouped together on one wall. There was a picture of her there, asleep
on the bed with her arms spread wide. She opened her mouth
in a slight gasp.

Outside, in the living-room, he heard her movements as he
prepared to garotte.

That night, Rebus had one of his nightmarish dreams again. A
long, lingering kiss was followed by an ejaculation, both in the
dream and in reality. He woke up immediately afterwards.
The breath of the kiss was still around him, hanging to him
like an aura. He shook his head clear of it. He needed a
woman. Remembering the party to come, he relaxed a little.
But his lips were dry. He padded into the kitchen and found a
bottle of lemonade. It was flat, but served the purpose. Then
he remembered that he was still drunk, and would have a

hangover if he wasn't careful. He poured himself three glass-
fuls of water and forced them down.

He was pleased to find that the pilot-light was still on. It was
like a good omen. When he slipped back into bed, he even
remembered to say his prayers. That would surprise the Big
Man upstairs. He would note it in his muckle book: Rebus
remembered me tonight. May give him a nice day tomorrow.
Amen.

## IX

Michael Rebus loved his BMW as dearly as he loved life itself,
perhaps more so. As he sped down the motorway, the traffic to
his left hardly appearing to move at all, he felt that his car *was*
life in a strange, satisfying sort of way. He pointed its nose
towards the bright point of the horizon and let it forge towards that future, revving it hard, making no concessions to
anyone or anything.

That was the way he liked it; hard, fast luxury, push-button
and on-hand. He drummed his fingers on the leather of the
steering-wheel, toyed with the radio-cassette, eased his head
back onto the padded headrest. He dreamed often of just
taking off, leaving wife and children and house, just his car
and him. Taking off towards that far point, never stopping
except to eat and fill up the car, driving until he died. It
seemed like paradise, and so he felt quite safe fantasising
about it, knowing that he would never dare put paradise into
practice.

When he had first owned a car, he had wakened in the
middle of the night, opening his curtains to see if it was still
waiting for him outside. Sometimes he would rise at four or
five in the morning and take off for a few hours, astonished at
the distance he could cover so quickly, glad to be out on the
silent roads with only the rabbits and the crows for company,
his hand on the horn scaring fluttering clouds of birds into the

air. He had never lost that initial love-affair with cars, the manumission of dreams.

People stared at his car now. He would park it in the streets of Kirkcaldy and stand a little distance away, watching people envy that car. The younger men, full of bravado and expectancy, would peer inside, staring at leather and dials as though examining living things at the zoo. The older men, some with their wives in tow, would glance at the machine, sometimes spitting on the road afterwards, knowing that it represented everything they had wanted for themselves and failed to find. Michael Rebus had found his dream, and it was a dream he could watch any time he chose.

In Edinburgh, however, it depended where you parked as to whether your car would attract attention. He had parked on George Street one day, only to find a Rolls-Royce cruising to a stop behind him. He had keyed the ignition again, fuming, near-spitting. He had parked eventually outside a discotheque. He knew that parking an expensive car outside a restaurant or a discotheque would mean that a few people would mistake you for the owner of the particular set-up, and that thought pleased him immensely, erasing the memory of the Rolls-Royce and infusing him with new versions of the dream.

Stopping at traffic-lights, too, could be exciting, except when some half-arsed biker on a machine roared to a standstill behind him or, even worse, beside him. Some of those bikes were made for initial acceleration. More than once he had been beaten mercilessly in a race from traffic-lights. He tried not to think about those times either.

Today he parked where he had been told to park: in the car park atop Calton Hill. He could see over to Fife from his front window, and from the back he could see Princes Street laid out before him like a toy-set. The hill was quiet; it was not quite the tourist season, and it was cold. He knew that things hotted up at night: car chases, girls and boys hoping for a ride, parties at Queensferry beach. Edinburgh's gay community would mix with those merely curious or lonely, and a couple, hand-in-hand, would now and again enter the graveyard at the bottom of the hill. When darkness fell, the east end of Princes Street became a territory all of its own, to be passed around, to be shared. But he was not about to share his car with anyone. His dream was a fragile entity.

He watched Fife across the Firth of Forth, looking quite splendid from this distance, until the man's car slowed and stopped beside him. Michael slid across to his passenger seat and wound down the window, just as the other man was winding down his.

"Got the stuff?" he said.

"Of course," said the man. He checked in his mirror. Some people, a family of all things, had just come over the rise. "We better wait for a minute."

They paused, staring blankly at the scenery.

"No hassles across in Fife?" asked the man.

"None."

"The word's going round that your brother was over seeing you. Is that correct?" The man's eyes were hard; his whole being was hard. But the car he drove was a heap. Michael felt safe for the moment.

"Yes, but it was nothing. It was just the anniversary of our dad's death. That was all."

"He doesn't know anything?"

"Absolutely not. Do you think I'm thick or something?"

The man's glance silenced Michael. It was a mystery to him how this one man could invoke such fear in him. He hated these meets.

"If anything happens," the man was saying, "if *anything* goes wrong, you'll be in for it. I really mean that. Keep well clear of that bastard in future."

"It wasn't my fault. He just dropped in on me. He didn't even phone first. What could I do?"

His hands were gripping hard to the steering-wheel, cemented there. The man checked in his mirror again.

"All clear," he said, reaching behind him. A small package slipped through Michael's window. He took a look inside it, brought an envelope out of his pocket, and reached for the ignition.

"Be seeing you around, Mister Rebus," said the man, opening the envelope.

"Yes," said Michael, thinking: not if I can help it. This work was getting a bit too hairy for him. These people seemed to know everything about his movements. He knew, however, that the fear always evaporated, to be replaced by euphoria when he had ridden himself of another load, pocketing a nice profit on the deal. It was that moment when fear turned to euphoria that kept him in the game. It was like the fastest piece of acceleration from traffic-lights that you could experience—ever.

Jim Stevens, watching from the hill's Victorian folly, a ridiculous, never-completed copy of a Greek temple, saw Michael Rebus leave. That much was old news to him; he was more interested in the Edinburgh connection, a man he could not trace and did not know, a man who had lost him twice before and who could doubtless lose him again. Nobody seemed to know who this mysterious figure was, and nobody particularly wanted to know. He looked like trouble. Stevens, feeling suddenly impotent and old, could do nothing other than jot down the car registration number. He thought that perhaps McGregor Campbell could do something with it, but he was wary of being found out by Rebus. He felt trapped in the middle of something which was proving altogether a knottier problem than he had suspected.

Shivering, he tried to persuade himself that he liked it that way.

## X

"Come in, come in, whoever you are."

Rebus's coat, gloves, and bottle of wine were taken from him by complete strangers, and he was plunged into one of

those packed, smoky, loud parties where it is easy to smile at
people but near impossible to get to know anyone. He moved
from the hall into the kitchen, and from there, through a
connecting door, into the living-room itself.

The chairs, table, settee had been pushed back to the walls,
and the floor was filled with writhing, whooping couples, the
men tieless, their shirts sticking to them.

The party, it appeared, had started earlier than he had
anticipated.

He recognised a few faces around and beneath him, stepping over two inspectors as he waded into the room. He could
see that the table at the far end had bottles and plastic cups
heaped upon it, and it seemed as good a vantage point as any,
and safer than some.

Getting to it was the problem, however, and he was reminded of some of the assault courses of his Army days.

"Hi there!"

Cathy Jackson, doing a passable imitation of a rag-doll,
reeled into his path for a second before being swept off her
feet by the large—the very large—man with whom she was
pretending to dance.

"Hello," managed Rebus, his face twisting into a grimace
rather than a smile. He achieved the relative safety of the
drinks-table and helped himself to a whisky and a chaser. That
would do for starters. Then he watched as Cathy Jackson (for
whom he had bathed, polished, scraped, adjusted, and
sprayed) pushed her tongue into the cavernous mouth of her
dancing-partner. Rebus thought that he was going to be sick.
His partner for the evening had done a bunk before the evening had begun! That would teach him to be optimistic. So
what did he do now? Leave quietly, or try to pull a few words
of introduction out of his hat?

A stocky man, not at all a policeman, came from the
kitchen, and, cigarette in mouth, approached the table with a
couple of empty glasses in his hand.

"Bloody hell," he said to nobody in particular, rummaging
amongst the bottles, "this is all a bit grim, isn't it?"

"Yes, it is a bit."

Rebus thought to himself, well, there it is, I've done it now, I've spoken to someone. The ice is broken, so I may as well leave while the going's good.

But he did not leave. He watched as the man weaved his way quite expertly back through the dancers, the drinks as safe as tiny animals in his hands. He watched as another record pounded out of the invisible stereo system, the dancers recommenced their war-dance, and a woman, looking every inch as uncomfortable as he did, squeezed her way into the room and was pointed in the direction of Rebus's table.

She was about his own age, a little ragged around the edges. She wore a reasonably fashionable dress, he supposed (who was he to talk about fashion? his suit looked downright funereal in the present company), and her hair had been styled recently, perhaps as recently as this afternoon. She wore a secretary's glasses, but she was no secretary. Rebus could see that much by looking at her, by examining the way she handled herself as she picked her way towards him.

He held a Bloody Mary, newly-prepared, towards her.

"Is this okay for you?" he shouted. "Have I guessed right or wrong?"

She gulped the drink thankfully, pausing for breath as he refilled the tumbler.

"Thanks," she said. "I don't normally drink, but that was much appreciated."

Great, Rebus thought to himself, the smile never leaving his eyes, Cathy Jackson's out of her head (and her morals) on alcohol, and I'm landed with a TT. Oh, but that thought was unworthy of him, and did no justice to his companion. He breathed a quick prayer of contrition.

"Would you like to dance?" he asked, for his sins.

"You're kidding!"

"I'm not. What's wrong?"

Rebus, guilty of a streak of chauvinism, could not believe it.

She was a D.I. Moreover, she was Press Liaison Officer on the murder case.

"Oh," he said, "it's just that I'm working that case, too."

"Listen, John, if it keeps on like this, every policeman and policewoman in Scotland is going to be on the case. Believe me."

"What do you mean?"

"There's been another abduction. The girl's mother reported her missing this evening."

"Shit. Excuse my language."

They had danced, drunk, separated, met again, and were now old friends for the evening, it seemed. They stood in the hallway, a little way from the noise and chaos of the dance-floor. A queue for the flat's only toilet was becoming unruly at the end of the corridor.

Rebus found himself staring past Gill Templer's glasses, past all that glass and plastic, to the emerald-green eyes beyond. He wanted to tell her that he had never seen eyes as lovely as hers, but was afraid of being accused of cliché. She was sticking to orange juice now, but he had loosened himself up with a few more whiskies, not expecting anything special from the evening.

"Hello, Gill."

Rebus recognised the stocky man before them as the person he had spoken with at the drinks-table.

"Long time no see."

The man attempted to peck Gill Templer's cheek, but succeeded only in falling past her and butting the wall.

"Had a drop too much to drink, Jim?" said Gill, coolly.

The man shrugged his shoulders. He was looking at Rebus.

"We all have our crosses to bear, eh?"

A hand was extended towards Rebus.

"Jim Stevens," said the man.

"Oh, the reporter?"

Rebus accepted the man's warm, moist hand for a moment.

"This is Detective Sergeant John Rebus," said Gill.

Rebus noticed the quick flushing in Stevens's face, the startled eyes of a hare. He recovered quickly though, expertly.

"Pleased to meet you," he said. Then, motioning with his head, "Gill and I go back a long way, don't we, Gill?"

"Not as far as you seem to think, Jim."

He laughed then, glancing towards Rebus.

"She's just shy," he said. "Another girl murdered, I hear."

"Jim has spies everywhere."

Stevens tapped the side of his blood-red nose, grinning towards Rebus.

"Everywhere," he said, "and I *get* everywhere, too."

"Yes, spreads himself a little thin, does our Jim," said Gill, her voice sharp as a blade's edge, her eyes suddenly shrouded in glass and plastic, inviolable.

"Another press briefing tomorrow, Gill?" said Stevens, searching through his pockets for his cigarettes, lost long before.

"Yes."

The reporter's hand found Rebus's shoulder.

"A long way, me and Gill."

Then he was gone, his hand held back towards them as he retreated, waving without the necessity of acknowledgement, searching out his cigarettes, filing away John Rebus's face.

Gill Templer sighed, leaning against the wall where Stevens's failed kiss had landed.

"One of the best reporters in Scotland," she said, matter-of-factly.

"And your job is dealing with the likes of him?"

"He's not so bad."

An argument seemed to be starting in the living-room.

"Well," said Rebus, all smiles, "shall we phone for the police, or would you rather be taken to a little restaurant I know?"

"Is that a chat-up line?"

"Maybe. You tell me. After all, you're the detective."

"Well, whatever it is, Detective Sergeant Rebus, you're in luck. I'm starving. I'll get my coat."

Rebus, feeling pleased with himself, remembered that his own coat was lurking somewhere. He found it in one of the bedrooms, along with his gloves, and—a cracking surprise— his unopened bottle of wine. He pocketed this, seeing it as a divine sign that he would be needing it later.

Gill was in the other bedroom, rummaging through the pile of coats on the bed. Beneath the bedcovers, congress seemed to be taking place, and the whole mess of coats and bedclothes seethed and writhed like some gigantic amoeba. Gill, giggling through it all, found her coat at last and came towards Rebus, who smiled conspiratorially in the doorway.

"Goodbye, Cathy," she shouted back into the room, "thanks for the party."

There was a muffled roar, perhaps an acknowledgement, from beneath the bedclothes. Rebus, his eyes wide, felt his moral fibre crumbling like a dry cheese-biscuit.

In the taxi, they sat a little distance apart.

"So, do you and this Stevens character go back a long way?"

"Only in his memory." She stared past the driver at the sleek, wet road beyond. "Jim's memory can't be what it was. Seriously, we went out together once, and I do mean once." She held up a finger. "A Friday night, I think it was. A big mistake, it certainly was."

Rebus was satisfied with that. He began to feel hungry again.

By the time they reached the restaurant, however, it was closed—even to Rebus—so they stayed in the taxi and Rebus directed the driver towards his flat.

"I'm a dab hand at bacon sandwiches," he said.

"What a pity," she said. "I'm a vegetarian."

"Good God, you mean you eat no vegetables at all?"

"Why is it," acid seeping into her voice, "that carnivores always have to make a joke out of it? It's the same with men and women's lib. Why is that?"

"It's because we're afraid of them," said Rebus, quite sober now.

Gill looked at him, but he was watching from his window as the city's late-night drunks rolled their way up and down the obstacle-strewn hazard of Lothian Road, seeking alcohol, women, happiness. It was a never-ending search for some of them, staggering in and out of clubs and pubs and take-aways, gnawing on the packaged bones of existence. Lothian Road was Edinburgh's dustbin. It was also home to the Sheraton Hotel and the Usher Hall. Rebus had visited the Usher Hall once, sitting with Rhona and the other smug souls listening to Mozart's Requiem Mass. It was typical of Edinburgh to have a crumb of culture sited amidst the fast-food shops. A requiem mass and a bag of chips.

"So how is the old Press Liaison these days?"

They were seated in his rapidly tidied living-room. His pride and joy, a Nakamichi tape-deck, was tastefully broadcasting one of his collection of late-night-listening jazz tapes; Stan Getz or Coleman Hawkins.

He had rustled up a round of tuna fish and tomato sandwiches, Gill having admitted that she ate fish occasionally. The bottle of wine was open, and he had prepared a pot of freshly-ground coffee (a treat usually reserved for Sunday breakfasts). He now sat across from his guest, watching her eat. He thought with a small start that this was the first female guest since Rhona had left him, but then recalled, very vaguely, a couple of other one-nighters.

"Press Liaison is fine. It's not really a complete waste of time, you know. It serves a useful purpose in this day and age."

"Oh, I'm not knocking it."

She looked at him, trying to gauge how serious he was being.

"Well," she went on, "it's just that I know a lot of our colleagues who think that a job like mine is a complete waste of time and manpower. Believe me, in a case like this one it's absolutely crucial that we keep the media on *our* side, and that we let them have the information that we want made public *when* it needs to be made public. It saves a lot of hassle."

"Hear, hear."

"Be serious, you bastard."

Rebus laughed.

"I'm never anything other than serious. A one-hundred-percent policeman's policeman, that's me."

Gill Templer stared at him again. She had a real inspector's eyes: they worked into your conscience, sniffing out guilt and guile and drive, seeking give.

"And being a Liaison Officer," said Rebus, "means that you have to . . . liaise with the press quite closely, right?"

"I know what you're getting at, Sergeant Rebus, and as your superior, I'm telling you to stop it."

"Sir!" Rebus gave her a short salute.

He came back from the kitchen with a pot of coffee.

"Wasn't that a dreadful party?" said Gill.

"It was the finest party I have ever attended," said Rebus. "After all, without it, I might never have met you."

She roared with laughter this time, her mouth filled with a paste of tuna and bread and tomato.

"You're a nutter," she cried, "you really are."

Rebus raised his eyebrows, smiling. Had he lost his touch? He had not. It was miraculous.

Later, she need to go to the bathroom. Rebus was changing a tape, and realising how limited his musical tastes were. Who were these groups that she kept referring to?

"It's in the hall," he said. "On the left."

When she returned, more jazz was playing, the music at times almost too low to be heard, and Rebus was back in his chair.

"What's that room across from the bathroom, John?"

"Well," he said, pouring coffee, "it used to be my daughter's room, but now it's just full of junk. I never use it."

"When did your wife and you split up?"

"Not as long ago as we should have. I mean that seriously."

"How old is your daughter?" She sounded maternal now, domestic; no longer the acid single woman or the professional.

"Nearly twelve," he said. "Nearly twelve."

"It's a difficult age."

"Aren't they all."

When the wine was finished and the coffee was down to its last half-cup, one or the other of them suggested bed. They exchanged sheepish smiles and ritual promises about not promising anything, and, the contract agreed and signed without words, went to the bedroom.

It all started well enough. They were mature, had played this game before too often to let the little fumblings and apologies get to them. Rebus was impressed by her agility and invention, and hoped that she was being impressed by his. She arched her spine to meet him, seeking the ultimate and unobtainable ingress.

"John," pushing at him now.

"What is it?"

"Nothing. I'm just going to turn over, okay?"

He knelt up, and she turned her back to him, sliding her knees down the bed, clawing at the smooth wall with her fingertips, waiting. Rebus, in the slight pause, looked around at the room, the pale blue light shading his books, the edges of the mattress.

"Oh, a futon," she had said, pulling her clothes off quickly. He had smiled in the silence.

He was losing it.

"Come on, John. Come on."

He bent towards her, resting his face on her back. He had talked about books with Gordon Reeve when they had been captured. Talked endlessly, it seemed, reading to him from his memory. In close confinement, torture a closed door away. But they had endured. It was a mark of the training.

"John, oh, John."

Gill raised herself up and turned her head towards his,

seeking a kiss. Gill, Gordon Reeve, seeking something from him, something he couldn't give. Despite the training, despite the years of practice, the years of work and persistence.

"John?"

But he was elsewhere now, back inside the training camp, back trudging across a muddy field, the Boss screaming at him to speed up, back in that cell, watching a cockroach pace the begrimed floor, back in the helicopter, a bag over his head, the spray of the sea salty in his ears . . .

"John?"

She turned round now, awkwardly, concerned. She saw the tears about to start from his eyes. She held his head to her.

"Oh, John. It doesn't matter. Really, it doesn't."

And a little later: "Don't you like it that way?"

They lay together afterwards, he guiltily, and cursing the facts of the confusion and the fact that he had run out of cigarettes, she drowsily, caring still, whispering bits and pieces of her life-story to him.

After a while, Rebus forgot to feel guilty: there was nothing, after all, to feel guilty about. He felt merely the distinct lack of nicotine. And he remembered that he was seeing Sammy in six hours' time, and that her mother would instinctively know what he, John Rebus, had been up to these past few hours. She was cursed with a witch-like ability to see into the soul, and she had seen his occasional bouts of crying at very close quarters indeed. Partly, he supposed, that had been responsible for their break-up.

"What time is it, John?"

"Four. Maybe a little after."

He slid his arm from beneath her and rose to leave the room.

"Do you want anything to drink?" he said.

"What did you have in mind?"

"Coffee maybe. It's hardly worth going to sleep now, but if you feel sleepy, don't mind me."

"No, I'll take a cup of coffee."

Rebus knew from her voice, from its slurred growliness, that she would be fast asleep by the time he reached the kitchen.

"Okay," he said.

He made himself a cup of dark, sweet coffee and slumped into a chair with it. He turned on the living-room's small gas fire and began to read one of his books. He was seeing Sammy today, and his mind wandered from the story in front of him, a tale of intrigue which he could not remember having started. Sammy was nearly twelve. She had survived many years of danger, and now, for her, other dangers were imminent. The perverts in watch, the ogling old men, the teenage cock-fighters, would be supplemented by the new urges of boys her age, and boys she already knew as friends would become sudden and forceful hunters. How would she cope with it? If her mother had anything to do with it, she would cope admirably, biting in a clinch and ducking on the ropes. Yes, she would survive without her father's advice and protection.

The kids were harder these days. He thought back to his own youth. He had been Mickey's big brother, fighting battles for the two of them, going home to watch his brother coddled by his father. He had pushed himself further into the cushions on the settee, hoping to disappear one day. Then they'd be sorry. Then they'd be sorry . . .

At seven-thirty he went through to the musky bedroom, which smelt two parts sex to one part animal lair, and kissed Gill awake.

"It's time," he said. "Get up, I'll run you a bath."

She smelt good, like a baby on a fireside towel. He admired the shapes of her twisted body as they awoke to the thin, watery sunlight. She had a good body all right. No real stretch-marks. Her legs unscarred. Her hair just tousled enough to be inviting.

"Thanks."

She had to be at HQ by ten in order to co-ordinate the next press release. There could be no rest. The case was still growing like a cancer. Rebus filled the bath, wincing at the rim of grime around it. He needed a cleaning-lady. Perhaps he could get Gill to do it.

*Another unworthy thought, forgive me.*

Which brought him to think of church-going. It was another Sunday, after all, and for weeks he had been promising himself that he would try again, would find another church in the city and would try all over again.

He hated congregational religion. He hated the smiles and the manners of the Sunday-dressed Scottish Protestant, the emphasis on a communion not with God but with your neighbours. He had tried seven churches of varying denominations in Edinburgh, and had found none to be to his liking. He had tried sitting for two hours at home of a Sunday, reading the Bible and saying a prayer, but somehow that did not work either. He was caught; a believer outwith his belief. Was a personal faith good enough for God? Perhaps, but not *his* personal faith, which seemed to depend upon guilt and his feelings of hypocrisy whenever he sinned, a guilt assuaged only by public show.

"Is my bath ready, John?"

She re-tousled her hair, naked and confident, her glasses left behind in the bedroom. John Rebus felt his soul to be imperilled. Sod it, he thought, catching her around the hips. Guilt could wait. Guilt could always wait.

He had to mop up the bathroom floor afterwards, the empirical evidence that Archimedes' displacement of water had been proved once again. The bath-water had flowed like milk and honey, and Rebus had nearly drowned.

Still, he felt better now.

"Lord, I am a poor sinner," he whispered, as Gill dressed. She looked stern and efficient when she opened the front door, almost as if she had been on a twenty-minute official visit.

"Can we fix a date?" he suggested.

"We can," she replied, looking through her bag. Rebus was

curious to know why women always did that, especially in films and thrillers, after they had been sleeping with a man. Did women suspect their sleeping partners of rifling their purses?

"But it might be difficult," she continued, "the case going the way it is. Let's just promise to keep in touch, okay?"

"Okay."

He hoped that she took note of the dismay in his voice, the disappointment of the small boy at having his request denied.

They pecked a final kiss, mouths brittle by now, and then she was gone. Her scent remained, however, and he breathed it in deeply as he prepared for the day ahead. He found a shirt and a pair of trousers that didn't reek of tobacco, and these he put on slowly, admiring himself in the bathroom mirror, the soles of his feet damp, while he hummed a hymn.

Sometimes it was good to be alive. Sometimes.

## XI

Jim Stevens poured another three aspirin into his mouth and drank his orange juice. The ignominy of it, being seen in a Leith bar sucking on fruit juice, yet the idea of drinking even a half-pint of the rich, frothing beer made him feel nauseous. He had drunk far too much at that party; too much too quickly, and in too many combinations.

Leith was trying to improve itself. Someone somewhere had decided to give it a bit of a dust and a wash. It boasted French-style cafés and wine bars, studio flats, delicatessen. But it was still Leith, still the old port, an echo of its roaring, bustling past when Bordeaux wines would be unloaded by the gallon and sold on the streets from a horse and cart. If Leith retained nothing else, it would retain a port's mentality, and a port's traditional drinking-dens.

"By Christ," roared a voice behind him, "the man drinks everything in doubles, even his soft drinks!"

A heavy fist, twice the dimensions of his own, landed on

Stevens's back. The swarthy figure landed on a stool beside
him. The hand stayed firmly where it was.

"Hello, Podeen," said Stevens. He was starting to sweat in
the heavy atmosphere of the saloon, and his heart was pounding: terminal hangover symptoms; he could smell the alcohol
squeezing itself out of his pores.

"Lordy, James, me boy, what the hell's that you're supping?
Barman, get this man a whisky quick. He's wasting away on
kiddies' juice!"

With a roar, Podeen took his hand off the reporter's back
just long enough to relieve the pressure, before bringing it
back down again in a stinging back-slap. Stevens felt his insides shudder rebelliously.

"Anything I can do for you today?" said Podeen, his voice
much lower.

Big Podeen had been a sailor for twenty years, with the
scars and nicks of a thousand ports on his body. How he made
his money these days, Stevens did not wish to know. He did
some bouncing for pubs on Lothian Road and dubious drinking-dens around Leith, but that would be the tip of his earn-
ings iceberg. Podeen's fingers were so encrusted with dirt
that he might have carved out the black economy single-
handedly from the rotten, fertile soil beneath him.

"Not really, Big Man. No, I'm just mulling things over."

"Get me a breakfast, will you? Double helpings of everything."

The barman, almost saluting Podeen, went off to give the
order.

"See," said Podeen, "you're not the only man who orders
everything in doubles, eh, Jimmy?"

The hand was lifted from Stevens's back again. He gri-
maced, waiting for the slap, but the arm flopped onto the bar
beside him instead. He sighed, audibly.

"Rough night last night, was it, Jimmy?"

"I wish I could remember."

He had fallen asleep in one of the bedrooms, very late in the
evening. Then a couple had come in, and they had lifted him

into the bathroom, depositing him in the bath. There he had slept for two hours, maybe three. He had awakened with a terrific stiffness in his neck, back, and legs. He had drunk some coffee, but not enough, never enough.

And had walked in the chilled morning air, chatting in a newsagent's shop with some taxi-drivers, sitting in the porter's cubby-hole of one of the big hotels on Princes Street, supping sweet tea and talking football with the bleary night-porter. But he had known he would end up down here, for this was his morning off, and he was back on the drugs case, his own little baby.

"Is there much stuff around at the moment, Big?"

"Oh, now, that depends what you're looking for, Jimmy. Word's out that you're getting to be a bit too nosy in every department. Best if you were sticking to the safe drugs. Keep away from the big stuff."

"Is this a timely warning or a threat or what?" Stevens wasn't in the mood to be threatened, not when he had a Sunday morning hangover to sort out.

"It's a *friendly* warning, a warning from a friend."

"Who's the friend, Big?"

"Me, you silly sod. Don't be so suspicious all the time. Listen, there's a little cannabis around, but that's about it. Nobody brings the stuff into Leith any more. They land it on the Fife coast, or up by Dundee. Places the Customs men have all but disappeared from. And that's the truth."

"I know, Big, I know. But there *is* a delivery going on around here. I've seen it. I don't know what it is. Whether it's big stuff or not. But I've seen a handover. Very recently."

"How recent?"

"Yesterday."

"Where?"

"Calton Hill."

Big Podeen shook his head.

"Then it's nothing at all to do with anyone or anything I know, Jimmy."

Stevens knew the Big Man, knew him well. He gave out

good information, but it was only what was given to him by people who wanted Stevens to get to know about something. So the heroin boys would come across, via Big, with information about cannabis dealing. If Stevens took the story up, chances were the cannabis dealers would be caught. And that left the territory and the demand to the heroin boys. It was clever stuff, ploy and counter-ploy. The stakes were high, too. But Stevens was a clever player himself. He knew that there was a tacit understanding that he was never to aim for the really big players, for that would mean aiming for the city's businessmen and bureaucrats, the titled landowners, the New Town's Mercedes owners.

And that would never be allowed. So he was fed tidbits, enough to keep the presses rolling, the tongues wagging about what a terrible place Edinburgh was becoming. Always a little, never the lot. Stevens understood all that. He had been playing the game so long he hardly knew sometimes what side he was on. In the end, it hardly mattered.

"You don't know about it?"

"Nothing, Jimmy. But I'll nose around. See what's doing. Listen, though, there's a new bar opened up by the Mackay showroom. Know the one I mean?"

Stevens nodded.

"Well," went on Podeen, "it's a bar at the front, but it's a brothel at the back. There's a wee cracker of a barmaid does her stuff of an afternoon, if you're interested."

Stevens smiled. So a new boy was trying to move in, and the old boys, Podeen's ultimate employers, didn't like it. And so he, Jim Stevens, was being given enough information to close down the new boy if he liked. There was a nice headline-catcher in it certainly, but it was a one-day wonder.

Why didn't they just telephone the police anonymously? He thought he knew the answer to that one, though once it had puzzled him: they were playing the game by its old-fashioned rules, which meant no snitching, no grassing to the enemy. He was left to play the part of messenger-boy, but a messenger-boy with power built into the system. Just a little power, but more power than lay in doing things along the straight and narrow.

"Thanks, Big. I'll bear that in mind."

The food arrived then, great piles of curled, shining bacon, two soft, near-transparent eggs, mushrooms, fried bread, beans. Stevens kept his eyes to the bar, suddenly interested in one of the beer-mats, damp still from Saturday night.

"I'm going across to my table to eat this, okay, Jimmy?"

Stevens could not believe his good luck.

"Oh, fine, Big Man, fine."

"Cheers, then."

And with that he was left alone, only the ghost of a smell remaining. He noticed that the barman was standing opposite him. His hand, shiny with grease, was held out.

"Two pounds sixty," he said.

Stevens sighed. Put that one down to experience, he thought to himself as he paid, or to the hangover. The party had been worth it, however, for he had met John Rebus. And Rebus was friendly with Gill Templer. It was all becoming just a little confusing. But interesting, too. Rebus was certainly interesting, though physically he did not resemble his brother in the slightest. The man had looked honest enough, but how did you tell a bent copper from the outside? It was the inside that was rotten. So, Rebus was seeing Gill Templer. He remembered the night they had spent together, and shuddered. That, surely, had been his nadir.

He lit a cigarette, his second of the day. His head was still clotted, but his stomach felt a little more composed. He might even be getting hungry. Rebus looked a tough nut, but not as tough as he would have been ten years ago. At this moment he was probably in bed with Gill Templer. The bastard. The lucky bastard. His stomach turned a tiny somersault of chilled jealousy. The cigarette felt good. It poured life and strength back into him, or seemed to. Yet he knew that it was scooping him out, too, tearing his guts to shreds of darkened meat. The hell with it. He smoked because without cigarettes he couldn't think. And he was thinking now.

"Hey, give me a double here will you?"

The barman came over.

"Orange juice again?"

Stevens looked at him disbelievingly.

"Don't be daft," he said, "whisky, Grouse if that's what's in the Grouse bottle."

"We don't play those sorts of game here."

"I'm glad to hear it."

He drank the whisky and felt better. Then he began to feel worse again. He went to the toilet, but the smell in there made him feel even worse. He held himself over the sink and brought up a few bubbles of liquid, retching loudly but emptily. He had to get off the booze. He had to get off the ciggies. They were killing him, yet they were the only things keeping him alive.

He walked over to Big Podeen's table, sweating, feeling older than his years.

"That was a good breakfast, that was," said the hulk of a man, his eyes gleaming like a child's.

Stevens sat down beside him.

"What's the word on bent coppers?" he asked.

## XII

"Hello, daddy."

She was eleven, but looked and spoke and smiled older: eleven going on twenty-one. That was what living with Rhona had done to his daughter. He pecked her cheek, thinking back to Gill's leave-taking. There was perfume around her, and a hint of make-up on her eyes.

He could kill Rhona.

"Hello, Sammy," he said.

"Mummy says that I'm to be called Samantha now that I'm growing up so quickly, but I suppose it's all right for *you* to call me Sammy."

"Oh, well, mummy knows best, Samantha."

He cast a look towards the retreating figure of his wife, her body pressed, pushed, and prodded into a shape attainable only with the aid of some super-strong girdle. She was not, he was relieved to find, wearing as well as their occasional telephone conversations would have had him believe. She stepped into her car now, never looking back. It was a small and expensive model, but had a sizeable dent in one side. Rebus blessed that dent.

He recalled that, making love, he had gloried in her body, in the soft flesh—the padding, as she had called it—of her thighs and her back. Today she had looked at him with cold eyes, filled with a cloud of unknowing, and had seen in his eyes the gleam of sexual satisfaction. Then she had turned on her heels. So it was true: she could still see into his heart. Ah, but she had failed to see into his soul. She had missed that most vital organ completely.

"What do you want to do then?"

They were standing at the entrance to Princes Street Gardens, adjacent to the tourist haunts of Edinburgh. A few people wandered past the closed shops of a Princes Street Sunday, while others sat on benches in the gardens, feeding crumbs to the pigeons and the Canadian squirrels or else reading the heavy-printed Sunday papers. The Castle reared above them, its flag flying briskly in the all-too-typical breeze. The Gothic missile of the Scott Monument pointed religious believers in the right direction, but few of the tourists who snapped it with their expensive Japanese cameras seemed at all interested in the structure's symbolic connotations, never mind its reality, just so long as they had some snaps of it to show off to their friends back home. These tourists spent so much time photographing things that they never actually *saw* anything, unlike the young people milling around, who were too busy enjoying life to be bothered capturing false impressions of it.

"What do you want to do then?"

The tourist side of his capital city. They were never interested in the housing-estates around this central husk. They

never ventured into Pilton or Niddrie or Oxgangs to make an
arrest in a piss-drenched tenement; they were not moved by
Leith's pushers and junkies, the deft-handed corruption of
the city gents, the petty thefts of a society pushed so far into
materialism that stealing was the only answer to what they
thought of as their needs. And they were almost certainly
unaware (they were not, after all, here to read local newspapers and watch local TV) of Edinburgh's newest media star,
the child murderer the police could not catch, the murderer
who was leading the forces of law and order a merry dance
without a clue or a lead or a cat in hell's chance of finding him
until he slipped up. He pitied Gill her job. He pitied himself.
He pitied the city, right down to its crooks and bandits, its
whores and gamblers, its perpetual losers and winners.

"So what do you want to do?"

His daughter shrugged her shoulders.

"I don't know. Walk maybe? Go for a pizza? See a film?"

They walked.

John Rebus had met Rhona Phillips just after joining the police. He had suffered a nervous breakdown just prior to his
joining the force *(why did you leave the Army, John?)* and had
recuperated in a fishing-village on the Fife coast, though he
had never told Michael of his presence in Fife during that
time.

On his first holiday from police-work, his first proper *holiday* in years, the others having been spent on courses or
working towards examinations, Rebus had returned to that
fishing-village, and there had met Rhona. She was a schoolteacher, already with a brutally short and unhappy marriage
behind her. In John Rebus she saw a strong and able husband,
someone who would not flinch in a fight; someone she could
care for, too, however, since his strength failed to conceal an
inner fragility. She saw that he was haunted still by his years in
the Army, and especially by his time in "special services." He
would awake crying some nights, and sometimes would weep
as he made love, weeping silently, the tears falling hard and

slow on her breasts. He would not speak about it much, and she had never pushed him. She was aware that he had lost a friend during his training days. She understood that much, and he appealed to the child in her and to the mother. He seemed perfect. Too, too perfect.

He was not. He should never have married. They lived happily enough, she teaching English in Edinburgh until Samantha was born. Then, however, niggling fights and power-plays had turned into sourer, unabated periods of resentment and suspicion. Was she seeing another man, a teacher at her school? Was he seeing another woman when he claimed to be involved in his numerous double-shifts? Was she taking drugs without his knowledge? Was he taking bribes without hers? In fact, the answer to all of these suspicions was no, but that did not seem to be what was at stake in any case. Rather, something larger was looming, yet neither could perceive the inevitability of it until too late, and they would cuddle up and make things right between them over and over again, as though in some morality-tale or soap-opera. There was, they agreed, the child to think of.

The child, Samantha, had become a young woman, and Rebus felt his eyes straying appreciatively and guiltily (yet again) over her as they walked through the gardens, around the Castle, and up towards the ABC cinema on Lothian Road. She was not beautiful, for only women could be that, but she was growing towards beauty with a confident inevitability which was breathtaking in itself, and horrifying. He was, after all, her father. There had to be some feelings there. It went with the territory.

"Do you want me to tell you about mummy's new boy-friend?"

"You know damn well I do."

She giggled; still something of the girl left in her then, and yet even a giggle seemed different in her now, seemed more controlled, more womanly.

"He's a poet, supposedly, but really he hasn't had a book out or anything yet. His poems are crap, too, but mummy won't tell him that. She thinks the sun shines out of his you-know-where."

Was all this "adult" talk supposed to impress him? He supposed so.

"How old is he?" Rebus asked, flinching at his suddenly revealed vanity.

"I don't know. Twenty maybe."

He stopped flinching and started to reel. Twenty. She was cradle-snatching now. My God. What effect was all this having on Sammy? On Samantha, the pretend adult? He dreaded to think, but he was no psychoanalyst; that was Rhona's department, or once had been.

"Honest, though, dad, he's an *awful* poet. I've done better stuff than his in my essays at school. I go to the big school after the summer. It'll be funny to go to the school where mum works."

"Yes, won't it." Rebus had found something niggling him. A poet, aged twenty. "What's this boy's name?" he asked.

"Andrew," she said, "Andrew Anderson. Doesn't that sound funny? He's nice really, but he's a bit weird."

Rebus cursed under his breath: Anderson's son, the dreaded Anderson's itinerant poet son was shacked up with Rebus's wife. What an irony! He didn't know whether to laugh or cry. Laughter seemed marginally more appropriate.

"What are you laughing at, daddy?"

"Nothing, Samantha. I'm just happy, that's all. What were you saying?"

"I was saying that mum met him at the library. We go there a lot. Mum likes the literature books, but I like books about romances and adventures. I can never understand the books mum reads. Did you read the same books as her when you were . . . before you . . . ?"

"Yes, yes, we did. But I could never understand them either, so don't worry about it. I'm glad that you read a lot. What's this library like?"

"It's really big, but a lot of tramps go there to sleep and

spend a lot of time. They get a book and sit down and just fall asleep. They smell awful!"

"Well, you don't need to go near them, do you? Best to let them keep themselves to themselves."

"Yes, daddy." Her tone was slightly reproachful, warning him that he was giving fatherly advice and that such advice was unnecessary.

"Fancy seeing a film then, do you?"

The cinema, however, was not open, so they went to an ice-cream parlour at Tollcross. Rebus watched Samantha scoop five colours of ice-cream from a Knickerbocker Glory. She was still at the stick-insect stage, eating without putting on an ounce of weight. Rebus was conscious of his sagging waist-band, a stomach pampered and allowed to roam as it pleased. He sipped cappuccino (without sugar) and watched from the corner of his eye as a group of boys at another table looked towards his daughter and him, whispering and sniggering. They pushed back their hair and smoked their cigarettes as though sucking on life itself. He would have arrested them for self-afflicted growth-stunting had Sammy not been there.

Also, he envied them their cigarettes. He did not smoke when with Sammy: she did not like him smoking. Her mother also, once upon a time, had screamed at him to stop, and had hidden his cigarettes and lighter, so that he had made secret little nests of cigarettes and matches all around the house. He had smoked on regardless, laughing in victory when he saun-tered into the room with another lit cigarette between his lips, Rhona screeching at him to put the bloody thing out, chasing him around the furniture, her hands flapping to knock the incendiary from his mouth.

Those had been happy times, times of loving conflict.

"How's school?"

"It's okay. Are you involved in the murder case?"

"Yes." God, he could murder for a cigarette, could tear a young male head from its body.

"Will you catch him?"

"Yes."

"What does he do to the girls, daddy?" Her eyes, trying to seem casual, examined the near-empty ice-cream glass very scrupulously.

"He doesn't do anything to them."

"Just murders them?" Her lips were pale. Suddenly she was very much his child, his daughter, very much in need of protection. Rebus wanted to put his arms around her, to comfort her, to tell her that the big bad world was out there, not in here, that she was safe.

"That's right," he said instead.

"I'm glad that's all he does."

The boys were whistling now, trying to attract her attention. Rebus felt his face growing red. On another day, any day other than this, he would march up to them and ram the law into their chilled little faces. But he was off-duty. He was enjoying an afternoon out with his daughter, the freakish result of a single grunted climax, that climax which had seen a lucky sperm, crawling through the ooze, make it all the way to the winning-post. Doubtless Rhona would already be reaching over for her book of the day, her literature. She would prise the still, spent body of her lover from her without a word being passed between them. Was her mind on her books all the time? Perhaps. And he, the lover, would feel deflated and empty, a vacant space, but suddenly, as if no form of transference had taken place. That was her victory.

*And then he would scream at her with a kiss. The scream of longing, of his solitary.*

*Let me out. Let me out . . .*

"Come on, let's get out of here."

"Okay."

And as they passed the table of hankering boys, their faces full of barely-restrained lust, jabbering like monkeys, Samantha smiled at one of them. *She smiled at one of them.*

Rebus, sucking in fresh air, wondered what his world was coming to. He wondered whether his reason for believing in another reality behind this one might not be because the everyday was so frightening and so very sad. If this were all there was, then life was the sorriest invention of all time. He could kill those boys, and he wanted to smother his daughter, to protect her from that which she wanted—and would get. He realised that he had nothing to say to her, and that those boys did have; that he had nothing in common with her save blood, while they had everything in common with her. The skies were dark as Wagnerian opera, dark as a murderer's thoughts. Darkening like similes, while John Rebus's world fell apart.

"It's time," she said, by his side yet so much bigger than him, so much more full of life. "It's time."

And indeed it was.

"We better hurry," said Rebus, "it's going to rain."

He felt tired, and recalled that he had not slept, that he had been involved in strenuous labour throughout the short night. He took a taxi back to the flat—sod the expense—and crawled up the winding stairs to his front door. The smell of cats was overpowering. Inside his door, a letter, unstamped, awaited him. He swore out loud. The bastard was everywhere, everywhere and yet invisible. He ripped open the letter and read.

YOU'RE GETTING NOWHERE. NOWHERE. ARE YOU? SIGNED

But there was no signature, not in writing anyway. But inside the envelope, like some child's plaything, lay the piece of knotted twine.

"Why are you doing this, Mister Knot?" said Rebus, fingering the twine. "And just what are you doing?"

Inside, the flat was like a fridge: the pilot-light had blown out again.

# PART THREE

## *Knot*

### XIII

The media, sensing that the "Edinburgh Strangler" was not about to vanish in the night, took the story by its horns and created a monster. TV crews moved into some of the better hotel rooms in the city, and the city was happy enough to have them, it being not quite the tourist season yet.

Tom Jameson was as astute an editor as any, and he had a team of four reporters working on the story. He could not help noticing, however, that Jim Stevens was not on his best form. He seemed uninterested—never a good sign in a journalist. Jameson was worried. Stevens was the best he had, a household name. He would speak to him about it soon.

As the case grew along with the interest in it, John Rebus and Gill Templer became confined to communicating by telephone and via the occasional chance meeting in or around HQ. Rebus hardly saw his old station now. He was strictly a murder-case victim himself, and was told to think about nothing else during his waking hours. He thought about everything else: about Gill, about the letters, about his car's inability to pass its MOT. And all the time he watched Anderson, father of Rhona's lover, watched him as he grew ever more frantic for a motive, a lead, anything. It was almost a pleasure to watch the man in action.

As to the letters, Rebus had pretty much discounted his

wife and daughter. A slight mark on Knot's last missive had been checked by the forensic boys (for the price of a pint) and had turned out to be blood. Had the man nicked his finger while cutting the twine? It was yet another small mystery. Rebus's life was full of mysteries, not the least of which was where his ten legitimate daily cigarettes went. He would open his packet of a late afternoon, count the contents, and find that he was supposed to have smoked all ten of his ration already. It was absurd; he could hardly remember smoking one of the alloted ten, never mind all of them. Yet a count of the butts in his ashtray would produce empirical evidence enough to withstand any denials on his part. Bloody strange though. It was as though he were shutting out a part of his waking life.

He was stationed in the HQ's Incident Room at the moment, while Jack Morton, poor sod, was on door-to-door. From his vantage point he could see how Anderson was running the shambles. It was little wonder the man's son had turned out to be less than bright. Rebus also had to deal with the many phone-calls—from those of the trying-to-be-helpfuls to those of the psychic-cranks-who-want-to-confess— and with the interviews carried out in the building itself at all hours of the day and night. There were hundreds of these, all to be filed and put into some kind of order of importance. It was a huge task, but there was always the chance that a lead would come from it, so he was not allowed to slack.

In the hectic, sweaty canteen he smoked cigarette number eleven, lying to himself that it was from the next day's ration, and read the daily paper. They were straining for new, shocked adjectives now, having exhausted their thesauruses. The appalling, mad, evil crimes of The Strangler. This insane, evil, sex-crazed man. (They did not seem to mind that the killer had never sexually assaulted his victims.) Gymslip Maniac! "What are our police doing? All the technology in the world cannot replace the reassurance offered by bobbies on the beat. *We need them now.*" That was from James Stevens, our crime correspondent. Rebus remembered the stocky, drunk man from the party. He recalled the look on Stevens's face when he had been told Rebus's name. That was strange. Everything was bloody strange. Rebus put down the newspaper. Reporters. Again, he wished Gill well in her job. He studied the blurred photograph on the front of the tabloid. It showed a crop-haired, unintelligent child. She was grinning nervously, as though snapped at a moment's notice. There was a slight, endearing gap between her front teeth. Poor Nicola Turner, aged twelve, a pupil at one of the southside's comprehensive schools. She had no attachments to either of the other dead girls. There were no visible links between them, and what was more, the killer had moved up a year, choosing a High School kid this time. So there was to be no regularity about his choice of age-groups. The randomness continued unabated. It was driving Anderson nuts.

But Anderson would never admit that the killer had his beloved police force tied in knots. Tied in absolute knots. Yet there *had* to be clues. There had to be. Rebus drank his coffee and felt his head spin. He was feeling like the detective in a cheap thriller, and wished that he could turn to the last page and stop all his confusion, all the death and the madness and the spinning in his ears.

Back in the Incident Room, he gathered together reports of phone-calls that had come in since he had left for his break. The telephonists were working flat out, and near them a telex-machine was almost constantly printing out some new piece of information thought useful to the case and sent on by other forces throughout the country.

Anderson pushed his way through the noise as if swimming in treacle.

"A car is what we need, Rebus. A car. I want all the sightings of men driving away with children collated and on my desk in an hour. I want that bastard's car."

"Yes, sir."

And he was off again, wading through treacle deep enough to drown any normal human being. But not Indestructible

Anderson, impervious to any danger. That made him a liability, thought Rebus, sifting through the piles of paper on his desk, which were meant to be in some system of order.

Cars. Anderson wanted cars, and cars he would have. There were swear-on-a-Bible descriptions of a man in a blue Escort, a white Capri, a purple Mini, a yellow BMW, a silver TR7, a converted ambulance, an ice-cream van (the telephone-caller sounding Italian and wishing to remain anonymous), and a great big Rolls-Royce with personalized number plates. Yes, let's put them all into the computer and have it run a check of every blue Escort, white Capri, and Rolls-Royce in Britain. And with all that information at our fingertips . . . then what? More door-to-door, more gathering of telephone-calls and interviews, more paperwork and bullshit. Never mind, Anderson would swim through it all, indomitable amidst all the craziness of his personal world, and at the end of it all he would come out looking clean and shiny and untouchable, like an advertisement for washing powder. Three cheers.

Hip hip.

Rebus had not enjoyed bullshit during his Army days either, and there had been plenty of it then. But he had been a good soldier, a very good soldier, when finally they had got down to soldiering. But then, in a fit of madness, he had applied to join the Special Air Squadron, and there had been very little bullshit there, and an incredible amount of savagery. They had made him run from the railway station to the camp behind a sergeant in his jeep. They had tortured him with twenty-hour marches, brutal instructors, the works. And when Gordon Reeve and he had made the grade, the SAS had tested them just that little bit further, just that inch too far, confining them, interrogating them, starving them, poisoning them, and all for a little piece of worthless information, a few words that would show they had cracked. Two naked, shivering animals with sacks tied over their heads, lying together to keep warm.

"I want that list in an hour, Rebus," called Anderson, walking past again. He would have his list. He would have his pound of flesh.

Jack Morton arrived back, looking foot-weary and not at all amused with life. He slouched across to Rebus, a sheaf of papers under his arm, a cigarette in the other hand.

"Look at this," he said, lifting his leg. Rebus saw the foot-long gash in the material.

"What happened to you then?"

"What do you think? I got chased by a great Alsatian, that's what happened to me. Will I get a penny for this? Will I hell."

"You could try claiming for it anyway."

"What's the point? I'd just be made to look stupid."

Morton dragged a chair across to the table.

"What are you working on?" he asked, seating himself with visible relief.

"Cars. Lots of them."

"Fancy a drink later on?"

Rebus looked at his watch, considering.

"Might do, Jack. Thing is, I'm hoping to make a date for tonight."

"With the ravishing Inspector Templer?"

"How did you know that?" Rebus was genuinely surprised.

"Come on, John. You can't keep that sort of thing a secret—not from policemen. Better watch your step, mind. Rules and regulations, you know."

"Yes, I know. Does Anderson know about this?"

"Has he said anything?"

"No."

"Then he can't, can he?"

"You'd make a good policeman, son. You're wasted in this job."

"You're telling me, dad."

Rebus busied himself with lighting cigarette number twelve. It was true, you couldn't keep anything secret in a police station, not from the lower ranks, anyway. He hoped Anderson and the Chief wouldn't find out about it, though.

"Any luck with the door-to-door?" he asked.

"What do you think?"

"Morton, you have an annoying habit of answering a question with another question."

"Have I? It must be all this work then, spending my days asking questions, mustn't it?"

Rebus examined his cigarettes. He found he was smoking number thirteen. This was becoming ridiculous. Where had number twelve gone?

"I'll tell you, John, there's nothing to be had out there, not a sniff of a lead. No one's seen anything, no one knows anything. It's almost like a conspiracy."

"Maybe that's what it is then, a conspiracy."

"And has it been established that all three murders were the work of a single individual?"

"Yes."

The Chief Inspector did not believe in wasting words, especially with the press. He sat like a rock behind the table, his hands clasped before him, Gill Templer on his right. Her glasses—an affectation really, her vision was near-perfect—were in her bag. She never wore them while on duty, unless the occasion demanded it. Why had she worn them to the party? They were like jewellery to her. She found it interesting, too, to gauge different reactions towards when she was and was not wearing them. When she explained this to her friends, they looked at her askance as if she were joking. Perhaps it all went back to her first true love, who had told her that girls who wore glasses seemed, in his experience, to be the best. That had been fifteen years ago, but she still saw the look on his face, the smile, the glint.

Everything was a game to Gill Templer, everything but the job. She had not become an Inspector through luck or looks, but through hard, efficient work and the will to climb as high as they would let her go. And now she sat with her Chief Inspector, who was a token presence at these gatherings. It was Gill who made up the handouts, who briefed the Chief Inspector, who handled the media afterwards, and they all knew it. A Chief Inspector might add weight of seniority to the proceedings, but Gill Templer it was who could give the journalists their "extras," the useful snippets left unsaid.

Nobody knew that better than Jim Stevens. He sat to the back of the room, smoking without removing the cigarette from his mouth once. He took little of the Chief Inspector's words in. He could wait. Still, he jotted down a sentence or two for future use. He was still a newsman after all. Old habits never died. The photographer, a keen teenager, nervously changing lenses every few minutes, had departed with his roll of film. Stevens looked around for someone he might have a drink with later on. They were all here. All the old boys from the Scottish press, and the English correspondents too. Scottish, English, Greek—it didn't matter, pressmen always looked like nothing other than pressmen. Their faces were robust, they smoked, their shirts were a day or two old. They did not look well-paid, yet were extremely well-paid, and with more fringe benefits than most. But they worked for their money, worked hard at building up contracts, squeezing into nooks and crannies, stepping on toes. He watched Gill Templer. What would she know about John Rebus? And would she be willing to tell? They were still friends after all, she and him. Still friends.

Maybe not good friends, certainly not good friends— though he had tried. And now she wanted Rebus . . . Wait until he nailed that bastard, if there *was* anything there to nail. Of course there was something there to nail. He could sense it. Then her eyes would be opened, truly opened. Then they would see what they would see. He was already preparing the headline. Something to do with "Brothers in Law— Brothers in Crime!" Yes, that had a nice ring to it. The Rebus brothers put behind bars, and all his own work. He turned his attention back to the murder case. But it was all too easy, too easy to sit down and write about police inefficiency, about the conjectured maniac. Still, it was bread and butter for the moment. And there was always Gill Templer to stare at.

"Gill!"

He caught her as she was getting into her car.

"Hello, Jim." Cold, business-like.

"Listen, I just wanted to apologise about my behaviour at the party." He was out of breath after a brief job across the car park, and the words came slowly from his burning chest. "I mean, I was a bit pissed. Anyway, sorry."

But Gill knew him too well, knew that this was merely a prelude to a question or a request. Suddenly she felt a little sorry for him, sorry for his fair, thick hair which needed a wash, sorry for his short, stocky—she had once thought it powerful—body, for the way he trembled now and again as though cold. But the pity soon wore off. It had been a hard day.

"Why wait till now to tell me? You could have said something at Sunday's briefing."

He shook his head.

"I didn't make Sunday's briefing. I was a bit hungover. You must have noticed I wasn't there?"

"Why should I have noticed that? Plenty of other people were there, Jim."

That cut him, but he let it pass.

"Well, anyway," he said, "sorry. Okay?"

"Fine." She made to step into her car.

"Can I buy you a drink or something? To cement the apology, so to speak."

"Sorry, Jim, I'm busy."

"Meeting that man Rebus?"

"Maybe."

"Look after yourself, Gill. That one might not be what he seems."

She straightened up again.

"I mean," said Stevens, "just take care, all right?"

He wouldn't say any more just yet. Having planted a seed of suspicion, he would give it time to grow. Then he would question her closely, and perhaps then she would be willing to tell. He turned away from her and walked, hands in pockets, towards the Sutherland Bar.

## XIV

At Edinburgh's Main Public Lending Library, a large, un-stuffy old building sandwiched between a bookshop and a bank, the tramps were settling down for a day's snoozing. They came here, as though waiting out fate itself, to wait out the few days of absolute poverty before their next amount of state benefit was due. This money they would then spend in a day (perhaps, if stretched, two days) of festivity: wine, women, and songs to an unappreciative public.

The attitudes of the library staff towards these down-and-outs ranged from the immensely intolerant (usually voiced by the older members of staff) to the sadly reflective (the youngest librarians). It was, however, a public library, and as long as the worldly-wise travellers picked up a book at the start of the day there was nothing that could be done about them, unless they became rowdy, in which case a security-man was quickly on the scene.

So they slept in the comfortable seats, sometimes frowned upon by those who could not help wondering if this was what Andrew Carnegie had in mind when he put up the finance for the first public libraries all those years ago. The sleepers did not mind these stares, and they dreamed on, though nobody bothered to inquire what it was they dreamed of, and no one thought them important.

They were not, however, allowed into the children's section of the library. Indeed, any browsing adult not dragging a child in tow was looked at askance in the children's section, and especially since the murders of those poor wee girls. The librarians talked about it amongst themselves. Hanging was the answer; they were agreed on that. And indeed, hanging was being discussed again in Parliament, as happens when-

ever a mass murderer emerges out of the shadows of civilized
Britain. The most oft-repeated statement amongst the people
of Edinburgh, however, did not concern hanging at all. It was
put cogently by one of the librarians: "But *here,* in Edinburgh!
It's unthinkable." Mass murderers belonged to the smoky
back streets of the South and the Midlands, not to Scotland's
picture-postcard city. Listeners nodded, horrified and sad
that this was something they all had to face, each and every
Morningside lady in her faded hat of gentility, every thug
who roamed the streets of the housing-estates, every lawyer,
banker, broker, shop-assistant and vendor of evening newspapers. Vigilante groups had been hastily set up and just as
hastily disbanded by the swiftly reacting police. This was not,
said the Chief Constable, the answer. Be vigilant by all means,
but the law was never to be taken into one's own hands. He
rubbed together his own gloved hands as he spoke, and some
newspapermen wondered if his subconscious were not washing its Freudian hands of the whole affair. Jim Stevens's editor
decided to put it thus: LOCK UP YOUR DAUGHTERS!, and left it
pretty much at that.

Indeed, the daughters *were* being locked up. Some of them
were being kept away from school by their parents, or were
under heavy escort all the way there and all the way back
home, with an additional check on their welfare at lunch-
time. The children's section of the Main Lending Library had
grown deathly quiet of late, so that the librarians there had
little to do with their days except talk about hanging and read
the lurid speculations in the British press.

The British press had cottoned onto the fact that Edinburgh had a rather less than genteel past. They ran reminders
of Deacon Brodie (the inspiration, it was said, behind Stevenson's Jekyll & Hyde), Burke and Hare, and anything else that
came to light in their researches, right down to the ghosts that
haunted a suspicious number of the city's Georgian houses.
These tales kept the imaginations of the librarians alive while
there was a lull in their duties. They made sure each to buy a
different paper, so that they could glean as many pieces of

information as possible, but were disillusioned by how often journalists seemed to swap a central story between them, so that an identical piece would appear in two or three different papers. It was as if a conspiracy of writers was at work.

Some children, however, did still come to the library. The vast majority of these were accompanied by mother, father, or minder, but one or two still came alone. This evidence of the foolhardiness of some parents and their offspring further disturbed the faint-hearted librarians, who would ask the children, appalled, where their mothers and fathers were.

Samantha rarely came to the library's children's section, preferring older books, but she did so today to get away from her mother. A male librarian came over to her as she pored over the most childish stuff.

"Are you here on your own, dear?" he said.

Samantha recognised him. He'd been working here ever since she could remember.

"My mum's upstairs," she said.

"I'm glad to hear it. Stick close to her, that's my advice."

She nodded, inwardly fuming. Her mother had given her a similar lecture only five minutes before. She wasn't a child, but no one seemed prepared to accept that. When the librarian went over to talk with another girl, Samantha took out the book she wanted and gave her ticket to the old lady librarian with the dyed hair, whom the children called Mrs. Slocum. Then she hurried up the steps to the library's reference section, where her mother was busy looking for a critical study of George Eliot. George Eliot, her mother had told her, was a woman who had written books of tremendous realism and psychological depth at a time when men were supposed to be the great realists and psychologists, and women were supposed to be for nothing but the housework. That was why she had been forced to call herself "George" to get published.

To counter these attempts at indoctrination, Samantha had brought from the children's section an illustrated book about a boy who flies away on a giant cat and has adventures in a fantasy land beyond his dreams. That, she hoped, would piss her mother off. In the reference section, a lot of people sat at desks, coughing, their coughs echoing around the hushed hall. Her mother, glasses perched on her nose, looking very much like a schoolteacher, argued with a librarian about some book she had ordered. Samantha walked between the rows of desks, glancing at what people were reading and writing. She wondered why people spent so much time reading books when there were other things to be doing. She wanted to travel round the world. Perhaps then she would be ready to sit in dull rooms poring over these old books. But not until then.

He watched her as she moved up and down the rows of desks. He stood with his face half to her, looking as if he were studying a shelf of books on angling. She wasn't looking around her, though. There was no danger. She was in her own little world, a world of her own design and her own rules. That was fine. All the girls were like that. But this one was with someone. He could see that. He took a book from the shelf and flicked through it. One chapter caught his eye, and turned his thoughts away from Samantha. It was a chapter dealing with fly-knotting. There were lots of designs for knots. Lots of them.

## XV

Another briefing. Rebus enjoyed the briefings now, for there was always the possibility that Gill would be present, and that afterwards they would be able to go for a cup of coffee together. Last night they had eaten late at a restaurant, but she had been tired and had looked at him strangely, quizzing him a little more even than usual with her eyes, not wearing her spectacles at first, but then slipping them on half-way through the meal.

"I want to see what I'm eating."

But he knew she could see well enough. The glasses were a

psychological strengthener. They protected her. Perhaps he was just being paranoid. Perhaps she had been tired merely. But he suspected something more, though he could not think what. Had he insulted her in some way? Snubbed her without realising? He was tired himself. They went to their separate flats and lay awake, wanting not to be alone. Then he dreamed the dream of the kiss, and awoke to the usual result, the sweat tainting his forehead, his lips moist. Would he awake to another letter? To another murder?

Now he felt lousy from lack of sleep. But still he enjoyed the briefing, and not just because of Gill. There was the inkling of a lead at long last, and Anderson was anxious to have it substantiated.

"A pale blue Ford Escort," said Anderson. Behind him sat the Chief Superintendent, whose presence seemed to be unnerving the Chief Inspector. "A pale blue Ford Escort." Anderson wiped his brow. "We have reports of such a car being seen in the Haymarket district on the evening when victim number one's body was found, and we have two sightings of a man and a girl, the girl apparently asleep, in such a car on the night that victim number three went missing." Anderson's eyes came up from the document before him to gaze, it seemed, into the eyes of every officer present. "I want this made top priority, or better. I want to know the ownership details of every blue Ford Escort in the Lothians, and I want that information *sooner* than possible. Now I know you've been working flat out as it is, but with a little extra push we can nail chummy before he does any more killing. To this end, Inspector Hartley has drawn up a roster. If your name's on it, drop what you're doing and get busy on tracing this car. Any questions?"

Gill Templer was scribbling notes in her tiny notepad, perhaps concocting a story for the press. Would they want to release this? Probably not, not straight away. They would wait first to see if anything came of the initial search. If nothing did, then the public would be asked to help. Rebus didn't fancy this at all: gathering ownership details, trekking out to the suburbs, and mass-interviewing the suspects, trying to "nose" whether they were probable or possible suspects, then perhaps a second interview. No, he did not fancy this at all. He fancied accompanying D.I. Templer back to his cave and making love to her. Her back was all he could see of her from his present vantage point by the door. He had been last into the room yet again, having stayed at the pub a little longer than anticipated. It had been a prior appointment, lunch (liquid) with Jack Morton. Morton told him about the slow, steady progress of the outdoor inquiry: four-hundred people interviewed, whole families checked and re-checked, the usual cranks and amoral groups examined. And not a jot of actual light had been thrown on the case.

But now they had a car, or at least thought they did. The evidence was tenuous, but it was there, the likeness of a fact, and that was something. Rebus felt a little proud of his own part in the investigation, for it had been his painstaking cross-referencing of sightings which had thrown up this slender link. He wanted to tell Gill all about it, then arrange a rendezvous for later in the week. He wanted to see her again, to see anybody again, for his flat was becoming a prison-cell. He would slouch home of a late evening or early morning, tip onto his bed, and sleep, not bothering these days to tidy or to read or to buy (or even steal) any foodstuffs. He had neither the time nor the energy. Instead, he ate from kebab-houses and chip-shops, early-morning bakeries and chocolate-dispensers. His face was becoming paler than usual, and his stomach groaned as though there were no skin left to distend. He still shaved and put on a tie, as a matter of necessary propriety, but that was about it. Anderson had noticed that his shirts were not as clean as they might have been, but had said nothing so far. For one thing, Rebus was in his good books, begetter of the lead, and for another, anyone could see that in Rebus's present mood he was likely to take a swing at any detractor.

The meeting was breaking up. There were no questions in anyone's mind except the obvious one: when do we start

cracking up? Rebus hovered just outside the door, waiting for
Gill. She came out in the last group, in quiet conversation
with Wallace and Anderson. The Superintendent had his arm
around her waist playfully, gently ushering her out of the
room. Rebus glared at the group, this motley crew of superior
officers. He watched Gill's face, but she did not seem to notice
him. Rebus felt himself slide back down the snake on the
board, right down to the bottom line again, back into the
heap. So this was love. Who was kidding who?

As the group of three walked up the corridor, Rebus stood
there like a jilted teenager and cursed and cursed and cursed.

He'd been let down again. Let down.

*Don't let me down, John. Please.*

*Please Please Please*

*And a screaming in his memory . . .*

He felt dizzy, his ears ringing with the sea. Staggering a
little, he caught hold of the wall, trying to take comfort in its
solidity, but it seemed to be throbbing. He breathed hard,
thinking back to his days on the rock-strewn beach, recovering from his breakdown. The sea had been in his ears then,
too. The floor adjusted itself slowly. People walked by quizzi-
cally, but no one stopped to help. Sod them all. And sod Gill
Templer, too. He could manage on his own. He could manage
on his own, God save him. He would be okay. All he needed
was a cigarette and some coffee.

But really he needed their pats on the back, their congratu-
lations at a job well done, their acceptance. He needed someone to assure him that it was all going to be all right.

He would be all right.

That evening, a couple of after-duty drinks under his belt
already, he decided to make a night of it. Morton had to go off
on some errand, but that was okay, too. Rebus didn't need
company. He walked along Princes Street, breathing in the
evening's promise. He was a free man after all, just as free as
any of the kids hanging about outside the hamburger bar.
They preened and joked and waited, waiting for what? He

knew what: waiting for the time to come when they could go home and sleep into tomorrow. He too was waiting, in his own way, killing time.

In the Rutherford Arms he met a couple of drinkers whom he knew from evenings like this just after Rhona had left him. He drank with them for an hour, sucking at the beer as though it were mother's milk. They talked about football, about horse-racing, about their jobs, and the whole scene brought tranquility to Rebus. It was a normal evening's conversation, and he embraced it greedily, throwing in his own snippets of news. But enough was as good as a feast, and he walked briskly, drunkenly out of the bar, leaving his friends with promises of another time, edging his way down the street towards Leith.

Jim Stevens, sitting at the bar, watched in the mirror as Michael Rebus left his drink on his table and went to the toilet. A few seconds later, the mystery man followed him inside, having been sitting at another table. It looked as though they were meeting to discuss the next swap-over, both seeming too casual to actually be carrying anything incriminating. Stevens smoked his cigarette, waiting. In less than a minute, Rebus reappeared, coming up to the bar for another drink.

John Rebus, pushing through the pub's swing-doors, could not believe his eyes. He slapped his brother on the shoulder.

"Mickey! What are you doing here?"

Michael Rebus nearly died at that moment. His heart leapt high into his throat, causing him to cough.

"Just having a drink, John." But he looked guilty as hell, he was sure of that. "You gave me a fright," he went on, trying to smile, "hitting me like that."

"A brotherly slap, that's all it was. What are you drinking?"

While the brothers were in conversation, the man slipped out of the toilet and walked out of the bar, his eyes never glancing left or right. Stevens watched him go, but had other things on his mind now. He could not let the policeman see him. He turned away from the bar, as if searching for a face amongst the people at the tables. Now he was sure. The policeman had to be in on it. The whole sequence of actions had been very slick indeed, but now he was sure.

"So you're doing a show down here?" John Rebus, cheered by his previous drinks, now felt that things were going right for a change. He was reunited with his brother for that drink they had always been promising themselves. He ordered whiskies with lager chasers. "This is a quarter-gill pub," he told Michael. "That's a decent size of a measure."

Michael smiled, smiled, smiled, as though his life depended upon it. His mind was racing and jumbled. The last thing he needed was another drink. If word of this got out, it would seem too unlikely to his Edinburgh connection, too unlikely. He, Michael, would have his legs broken for this if it ever was to get out. He had been warned. And what was John doing here anyway? He seemed complacent enough, drunk even, but what if it were all a set-up? What if his connection had already been arrested outside? He felt as he had when, as a child, he had stolen money from his father's wallet, denying the crime for weeks afterwards, his heart heavy with guilt.

Guilty, guilty, guilty.

John Rebus meantime drank on and chatted, unaware of the sudden change of atmosphere, the sudden interest in him. All he cared about was the whisky in front of him and the fact that Michael was about to go off and do a show at a local bingo hall.

"Mind if I come along?" he asked. "I might as well see how my brother earns his crust."

"Sure," said Michael. He toyed with the whisky glass. "I'd better not drink this, John. I've got to keep my mind clear."

"Of course you have. Need to let the mysterious sensations flood over you." Rebus made an action with his hands as though hypnotising Michael, his eyes wide, smiling.

And Jim Stevens picked up his cigarettes and, his back to them still, left the smoky, noisy public house. If only it had been quieter in there. If only he could have heard what they were saying. Rebus saw him go.

"I think I know him," he told Michael, gesturing towards the door with his head. "He's a reporter on the local rag."

Michael Rebus tried to smile, smile, smile, but it seemed to him that his world was falling apart.

The Rio Grande Bingo Hall had been a cinema. The front twelve rows of seats had been taken out and bingo boards and stools put in their place, but to the back of these were still many rows of dusty, red seats, and the balcony seating was completely intact. John Rebus said that he preferred to sit upstairs, so that he would not distract Michael. He followed an elderly man and his wife upstairs. The seats looked comfortable, but as he eased himself into the second row, Rebus felt springs jar against his buttocks. He moved around a little, trying to get comfortable, and settled finally for a position where one cheek supported most of his weight.

There seemed a good enough crowd downstairs, but up here in the gloom of the neglected balcony there were only the old couple and himself. Then he heard shoes tapping on the aisle. They paused for a second, before a hefty woman slid into the second row. Rebus was forced to look up, and saw her smiling at him.

"Mind if I sit here?" she said. "Not waiting for anyone, are you?"

Her look was hopeful. Rebus shook his head, smiling politely. "Thought not", she said, sitting down beside him. And he smiling. He had never seen Michael smile so much, or so uneasily. Was it so embarrassing for him to meet his elder brother? No, there had to be more to it than that. Michael's had been the smile of the small-time thief, caught yet again. They needed to talk.

"I come here a lot to the bingo. But I thought this might be a good laugh, you know. Ever since my husband died," meaningful pause, "well, it's not been the same. I like to get out now and again, you know. Everybody does, don't they? So I thought I'd come along. Don't know what made me come upstairs. Fate, I suppose." Her smile broadened. Rebus smiled back.

She was in her early forties, a little too much make-up and scent, but quite well-preserved. She talked as if she had not spoken to anyone in days, as if it were important for her to establish that she could still speak and be listened to and understood. Rebus felt sorry for her. He saw a little of himself in her; not much, but almost enough.

"So what are you doing here?" She was forcing him to speak.

"Just here for the show, same as you are." He didn't dare say that his brother was the hypnotist. That would have left too many avenues for a response.

"You like this sort of thing, do you?"

"I've never been before."

"Neither have I." She smiled again, conspiratorially this time. She had found that they had something in common. Thankfully, the lights were going down—what lighting there was—and a spot had come up on the stage. Someone was introducing the show. The woman opened her handbag and produced a noisy bag of boiled sweets. She offered one to Rebus.

Rebus found himself, to his own surprise, enjoying the show, but not half as much as the woman beside him was. She howled with laughter as one willing participant, his trousers left on the stage, pretended to swim up and down the aisles. Another guinea-pig was made to believe that he was ravenously hungry. Another that she was a professional striptease artiste at one of her bookings. Another that he was falling asleep.

Still enjoying the show, Rebus began to nod off himself. It was the effect of too much alcohol, too little sleep, and the warm, broody darkness of the theatre. Only the final applause of the audience awoke him. Michael, sweating in his glittery stage suit, took the applause as though addicted to it, coming back for another bow when most of the people were leaving their seats. He had told his brother that he had to get home quickly, that he would not see him after the show, that he would phone him sometime for his reaction.

And John Rebus had slept through much of it.

He felt refreshed, however, and could hear himself accepting the perfumed woman's offer of a "one-for-the-road" drink at a local bar. They left the theatre arm-in-arm, smiling at something. Rebus felt relaxed, a child again. This woman was treating him like her son, really, and he was happy enough to be coddled. A final drink, and then he'd go home. Just one drink.

Jim Stevens watched them leave the theatre. It was becoming very strange indeed. Rebus seemed to be ignoring his brother now, and he had a woman with him. What did it all mean? One thing it meant was that Gill should be told about it at some opportune moment. Stevens, smiling, added it to his collection of such moments. It had been a good night's work so far.

So where in the evening had mother-love changed into physical contact? In that pub, perhaps, where her reddened fingers had bitten into his thigh? Outside in the cooling air when he wrapped his arms around her neck in a fumbled attempt at a kiss? Or here in her musty flat, smelling still of her husband, where Rebus and she lie across an old settee and exchanged tongues?

No matter. It's too late to regret anything, and too early. So he slouches after her when she retires to her bedroom. He tumbles into the huge double-bed, springy and covered in thick blankets and quilts. He watches her undress in darkness. The bed feels like one he had as a kid, when a hot-water-bottle was all he had to keep the chill off, and mounds of gritty blankets, puffed-out quilts. Heavy and suffocating, tiring in themselves.

No matter.

Rebus did not enjoy the particulars of her heavy body, and was forced to think of everything in the abstract. His hands on her well-suckled breasts reminded him of late nights with

Rhona. Her calves were thick, unlike Gill's, and her face was worn with too much living. But she was a woman, and she was with him, so he squeezed her into an abstract and tried to make them both happy. But the heaviness of the bedding oppressed him, caging him, making him feel small and trapped and isolated from the world. He fought against it, fought against the memory of Gordon Reeve and he as they sat in solitary, listening to the screams of those around them, but enduring, always enduring, and reunited finally. Having won. Having lost. Lost everything. His heart was pounding to her grunts, now some distance away it seemed. He felt the first wave of that absolute repulsion hit him in the stomach like a truncheon, and his hands slid around the hanging, yielding throat beneath him. The moans were inhuman now, catlike, keening. His hands pushed a little, the fingers finding their own purchase against skin and sheet. They locked him up and they threw away the key. They pushed him to his death and they poisoned him. He should not have been alive. He should have died back then, back in the rank, animal cells with their power-hoses and their constant questionings. But he had survived. He had survived. And he was coming.

*He alone, all alone*
*And the screaming*
*Screaming*

Rebus became aware of the gurgling sounds beneath him just before his head started to fry. He fell over onto the gasping figure and lost consciousness. It was like a switch being flipped.

## XVI

He awoke in a white room. It reminded him very much of the hospital room in which he had awoken after his nervous breakdown all those years ago. There were muffled noises from outside. He sat up, his head throbbing. What had happened? Christ, that woman, that poor woman. He had tried to kill her! Drunk, way too drunk. Merciful God, he had tried to strangle her, hadn't he? Why in God's name had he done that? Why?

A doctor pushed open his door.

"Ah, Mister Rebus. Good, you're awake. We're about to move you into one of the wards. How do you feel?"

His pulse was taken.

"Simple exhaustion, we think. Simple nervous exhaustion. Your friend who called for the ambulance—"

"My friend?"

"Yes, she said that you just collapsed. And from what we can gather from your employers, you've been working pretty hard on this dreadful murder hunt. Simple exhaustion. What you need is a break."

"Where's my . . . my friend?"

"No idea. At home, I expect."

"And according to her, I just collapsed?"

"That's right."

Rebus felt immediate relief flooding through him. She had not told them. She had not told them. Then his head began to pulse again. The doctor's wrists were hairy and scrubbed clean. He slipped a thermometer into Rebus's mouth, smiling. Did he know what Rebus had been doing prior to the blackout? Or had his friend dressed him before calling the ambulance? He had to contact the woman. He didn't know where she stayed, not exactly, but the ambulancemen would know, and he could check.

Exhaustion. Rebus did not feel exhausted. He was beginning to feel rested and, though slightly unnerved, quite unworried about life. Had they given him anything while he was asleep?

"Can I see a newspaper?" he muttered past the thermometer.

"I'll get an orderly to fetch you one. Is there anyone you wish us to contact? Any close relative or friend?"

Rebus thought of Michael.

"No," he said, "there's nobody to contact. All I want is a newspaper."

"Fair enough." The thermometer was removed, the details noted.

"How long do you want to keep me in here?"

"Two or three days. I may want you to see an analyst."

"Forget the analyst. I'll need some books to read."

"We'll see what we can do."

Rebus settled back then, having decided to let things take their course. He would lie here, resting though he needed no rest, and would let the rest of them worry about the murder case. Sod them all. Sod Anderson. Sod Wallace. Sod Gill Templer.

But then he remembered his hands slipping around that ageing throat, and he shivered. It was as though his mind were not his own. Had he been about to kill that woman? Should he see the analyst after all? The questions made his headache worse. He tried not to think about anything at all, but three figures kept coming back to him: his old friend Gordon Reeve, his new lover Gill Templer, and the woman he had betrayed her for, and nearly strangled. They danced in his head until the dance became blurred. Then he fell asleep.

"John!"

She walked quickly to his bed, fruit and vitamin-drink in her hands. She had make-up on her face, and was wearing strictly off-duty clothes. She pecked his cheek, and he could smell her French perfume. He could also see down the front of her silk blouse. He felt a little guilty.

"Hello, D.I. Templer," he said. "Here," lifting one edge of the bedcover, "get in."

She laughed, dragging across a stern-looking chair. Other visitors were entering the ward, their smiles and quiet voices redolent of illness, an illness Rebus did not feel.

"How are you, John?"

"Terrible. What have you brought me?"

"Grapes, bananas, diluting orange. Nothing very imaginative, I'm afraid."

Rebus picked a grape from the bunch and popped it into his mouth, setting aside the trashy novel in which he had been painfully involved.

"I don't know, Inspector, the things I have to do to get a date with you." Rebus shook his head wearily. Gill was smiling, but nervously.

"We were worried about you, John. What happened?"

"I fainted. In the home of a friend, by all accounts. It's nothing very serious. I have a few weeks to live."

Gill's smile was warm.

"They say it's overwork." Then she paused. "What's all this 'Inspector' stuff?"

Rebus shrugged, then looked sulky. His guilt was mixing with the remembrance of that snub he had been given, that snub which had started the whole ball rolling. He turned into a patient again, weakly slumping against his pillow.

"I'm a very ill man, Gill. Too ill to answer questions."

"Well, in that case I won't bother to slip you the cigarettes sent by Jack Morton."

Rebus sat up again.

"Bless that man. Where are they?"

She brought two packs from her jacket pocket and slipped them beneath the bedclothes. He gripped her hand.

"I missed you, Gill." She smiled, and did not withdraw the hand.

Limitless visiting-time being a prerogative of the police, Gill stayed for two hours, talking about her past, asking him about his own. She had been born on an air-force base in Wiltshire, just after the war. She told Rebus that her father had been an engineer in the RAF.

"My dad," Rebus said, "was in the Army during the war. I was conceived while he was on one of his last leaves. He was a stage hypnotist by profession." People usually raised an eyebrow at that, but not Gill Templer. "He used to work the music-halls and theatres, doing summer stints in Blackpool and Ayr and places like that, so we were always sure of a summer holiday away from Fife."

She sat with her head cocked to one side, content to be told stories. The ward was quiet once the other visitors had obeyed the leaving-bell. A nurse pushed around a trolly with a huge, battered pot of tea on it. Gill was given a cup, the nurse smiling at her in sisterhood.

"She's a nice kid, that nurse," said Rebus, relaxed. He had been given two pills, one blue and one brown, and they were making him drowsy. "She reminds me of a girl I knew when I was in the Paras."

"How long were you in the Paras, John?"

"Six years. No, eight years it was."

"What made you leave?"

What made him leave? Rhona had asked him the same question over and over, her curiosity piqued by the feeling that he had something to hide, some monstrous skeleton in his closet.

"I don't know really. It's hard to remember that far back. I was picked for special training and I didn't like it."

And this was the truth. He had no use for memories of his training, the reek of fear and mistrust, the screaming, that screaming in his memory. *Let me out.* The echo of solitary.

"Well," said Gill, "if *my* memory serves me right, I've got a case waiting for me back at base-camp."

"That reminds me," he said, "I think I saw your friend last night. The reporter. Stevens, wasn't it? He was in a pub the same time I was. Strange."

"Not so very strange. That's his kind of hunting-ground. Funny, he's a bit like you in some ways. Not as sexy though." She smiled and pecked his cheek again, rising from the metal chair. "I'll try to drop in again before they let you out, but you know what it's like. I can't make any concrete promises, D.S. Rebus."

Standing, she seemed taller than Rebus had imagined her. Her hair fell forward onto his face for another kiss, full on the lips this time, and he staring at the dark cleft between her breasts. He felt a little tired, so tired. He forced his eyes to remain open while she walked away, her heels clacking on the tiled floor while the nurses floated past like ghosts on their rubber-soled shoes. He pushed himself up so that he could watch her legs retreat. She had nice legs. He had remembered that much. He remembered them gripping his sides, the feet resting on his buttocks. He remembered her hair falling across the pillow like a Turner seascape. He remembered her voice hissing in his ears, that hissing. Oh yes, John, oh, John, yes, yes, yes.

*Why did you leave the army?*

As she turned over, turning into the woman with the choking cries of his climax.

*Why did you?*

Oh, oh, oh, oh.

Oh yes, the safety of dreams.

## XVII

The editors loved what the Edinburgh Strangler was doing for the circulations of their newspapers. They loved the way his story grew almost organically, as though carefully nurtured. The *modus operandi* had altered ever so slightly for the killing of Nicola Turner. The Strangler had, it seemed, tied a knot in the cord prior to strangulation. This knot had pressed heavily on the girl's throat, bruising it. The police did not consider this of much significance. They were too busy checking through the records of blue Ford Escorts to be busy with a slight detail of technique. They were out there checking every blue Escort in the area, questioning every owner, every driver.

Gill Templer had released details of the car to the press, hoping for a huge public response. It came: neighbours reported their neighbours, father their sons, wives their husbands, and husbands their wives. There were over two-hundred blue Escorts to investigate, and if nothing came of that, they would be re-investigated, before moving on to other colours of Ford Escort, other makes of light-blue saloon car. It might take months; certainly it would take weeks.

Jack Morton, another xeroxed list folded in his hand, had consulted his doctor about swollen feet. The doctor had told him that he walked too much in cheap, unsupportive shoes. This Morton already knew. He had now interviewed so many suspects that it was all becoming a blur to him. They all looked the same and acted the same: nervous, deferential, innocent. If only the Strangler would make a mistake. There were no clues worth going on. Morton suspected the car to be a false trail. No clues worth going on. He remembered John Rebus's anonymous letters. *There are clues everywhere.* Could that be true of this case? Could the clues be too big to notice, or too abstract? Certainly it was a rare—an extraordinarily rare— murder case that did not have some bumper, extravagant clue lying about somewhere just waiting to be picked up. He was damned if he knew where this one was though, and that was why he had visited his doctor—hoping for some sympathy and a few days off. Rebus had landed on *his* feet again, lucky sod. Morton envied him his illness.

He parked his car on a double-yellow line outside the library and sauntered in. The great front hall reminded him of the days when he had used this library himself, clutching picture-books borrowed from the children's section. It used to be situated downstairs. He wondered if it still was. His mother would give him the bus-fare, and he would come into town, ostensibly to change his library books, but really so that he could wander the streets for an hour or two, savouring the taste of what it would be like to be grown up and free. He would trail American tourists, taking note of their swaggering self-confidence and their bulging wallets and waistbands. He would watch them as they photographed Greyfriar's Bobby's statue across from the Kirkyard. He had stared long and hard at the statue of the small dog, and had felt nothing. He had read of Covenanters, of Deacon Brodie, of public executions on the High Street, wondering what kind of city this was, and

what kind of country. He shook his head now, past caring
about fantasies, and went to the information desk.

"Hello, Mister Morton."

He turned to find a girl, more a young lady really, standing
before him, a book clasped to her small chest. He frowned.

"It's me, Samantha Rebus."

His eyes went wide.

"Goodness, so it is. Well, well. You've certainly grown since
I last saw you. Mind you, that must have been a year or two
back. How are you?"

"I'm fine, thanks. I'm here with my mother. Are you here
on police business?"

"Something like that, yes." Morton could feel her eyes
burning into him. God, she had her father's eyes all right. He
had left his mark.

"How's dad keeping?"

To tell or not to tell. Why not tell her? Then again, was it his
place to tell her?

"He's fine, so far as I know," he said, knowing this to be
seventy-percent truth.

"I'm just going down to the teenagers' section. Mum's in
the Reference Room. It's dead boring in there."

"I'll go with you. That's just where I was headed."

She smiled at him, pleased about something that was going
on in her adolescent head, and Jack Morton had the thought
that she wasn't at all like her father. She was far too nice and
polite.

A fourth girl was missing. The outcome seemed a foregone
conclusion. No bookie would have given odds.

"We need special vigilance," stressed Anderson. "More officers are being drafted in tonight. Remember," the officers
present looked hollow-eyed and demoralized, "if and when
he kills this victim, he will attempt to dispose of the body, and
if we can spot him doing that, or if any member of the public
can spot him doing that, just once, then we've got him."
Anderson slapped a fist into his open hand. Nobody seemed

very cheered. So far the Strangler had dumped three corpses, quite successfully, in different areas of the city: Oxgangs, Haymarket, Colinton. The police could not be everywhere (though these days it seemed to the public that they were), no matter how hard they tried.

"Again," continued the Chief Inspector, consulting a file, "the recent abduction seems to have little enough in common with the others. The victim's name is Helen Abbot. Eight years of age, a bit younger than the others, you'll notice, light-brown shoulder-length hair. Last seen with her mother in a Princes Street store. The mother says that the girl simply disappeared. One minute there, the next minute gone, as was the case with the second victim."

Gill Templer, thinking this over later, found it curious. The girls could not themselves have been abducted actually in the shops. That would have been impossible without screams, without witnesses. One member of the public had come forward to say that a girl resembling Mary Andrews—the second victim—had been seen by him climbing the steps from the National Gallery up towards The Mound. She had been alone, and had seemed happy enough. In which case, Gill mused, the girl had sneaked away from her mother. But why? For some secret rendezvous with someone she had known, someone who had turned out to be her killer? In that case, it seemed likely that *all* the girls had known their murderer, so they *had* to have something in common. Different schools, different friends, different ages. What was the common denominator?

She admitted defeat when her head started to hurt. Besides, she had reached John's street and had other things to think about. He had sent her here to collect some clean clothes for his release, and to see if there were any mail, as well as checking that the central heating was working still. He had given her his key, and as she climbed the stairs, pinching her nose against the pervasive smell of cats, she felt a bond between John Rebus and herself. She wondered if the relationship were about to turn serious. He was a nice man, but a little hung-up, a little secretive. Maybe that was what she liked.

She opened his door, scooped up the few letters lying on the hall-carpet, and made a quick tour of the flat. Standing by the bedroom door, she recalled the passion of that night, the odour of which seemed to cling in the air still.

The pilot-light was lit. He would be surprised to learn that. What a lot of books he had, but then his wife had been an English teacher. She lifted some of them off the floor and arranged them on the empty shelves of the wall-unit. In the kitchen, she made herself some coffee and sat down to drink it black, looking over the mail. One bill, one circular, and one typed letter, posted in Edinburgh and three days ago at that. She stuffed the letters into her bag and went to inspect the wardrobe. Samantha's room, she noted, was still locked. More memories pushed safely away. Poor John.

Jim Stevens had far too much work to do. The Edinburgh Strangler was proving himself a meaty individual. You couldn't ignore the bastard, even if you felt you had better things to do. Stevens had a staff of three working with him on the newspaper's daily reports and features. Child abuse in Britain today was the flavour of tomorrow's piece. The figures were horrifying enough, but more horrifying yet was the sense of biding time, waiting for the dead girl to turn up. Waiting for the next one to go missing. Edinburgh was a ghost town. Children were kept indoors, those allowed out scuttling through the streets like creatures under chase. Stevens wanted to turn his attentions to the drugs case, the mounting evidence, the police connection. He wanted to, but there simply was not the time. Tom Jameson was on his back every hour of the day, roaming through the office. Where's that copy, Jim? It's about time you earned your keep, Jim. When's the next briefing, Jim? Stevens was burned out by the end of each and every day. He decided that his work on the Rebus case had to stop for the moment. Which was a pity, because with the police at full stretch working on the murders, the field was left wide open for any and all other crimes, including pushing drugs. The Edinburgh Mafia must be having a field-day. He had used the story of the Leith "bordello," hoping for some information in return, but the big boys appeared not to be playing. Well, sod them. His time would come.

When she arrived in the ward, Rebus was reading through a Bible, courtesy of the hospital. When the Sister had found out about his request, she had asked him if he wished to speak to a priest or a minister, but this offer he had declined strenuously. He was quite content—more than content—to flick through some of the better passages in the Old Testament, refreshing his memory of their power and their moral strength. He read the stories of Moses, Samson, and David, before coming to the Book of Job. Here he found a power he could not remember having encountered before:

> When an innocent man suddenly dies, God laughs.
> God gave the world to the wicked.
> He made all the judges blind.
> And if God didn't do it, who did?

> If I smile and try to forget my pain,
> All my suffering comes back to haunt me;
> I know that God does hold me guilty.
> Since I am held guilty, why should I bother?
> No soap can wash away my sins.

Rebus felt his spine shiver, though the ward itself was oppressively warm, and his throat cried out for water. As he poured some of the tepid liquid into a plastic beaker, he saw Gill coming towards him on quieter heels than previously. She was smiling, bringing what joy there was into the ward with her. A few of the men eyed her appreciatively. Rebus felt glad, all of a sudden, to be leaving this place today. He put the Bible aside and greeted her with a kiss on the nape of her neck.

"What have you got there?"

He took the parcel from her and found it to contain his change of clothes.

"Thanks," he said. "I didn't think this shirt was clean, though."

"It wasn't." She laughed and pulled across a chair. "Nothing was. I'd to wash and iron all your clothes. They constituted a health hazard."

"You're an angel," he said, putting the parcel aside. "Speaking of which, what were you reading in the book?" She tapped the red, fake-leather binding of the Bible.

"Oh, nothing much. Job, actually. I read it once a long time ago. It seems more frightening now, though. The man who begins to doubt, who shouts out against his God, looking for a response, and who gets one. 'God gave the world to the wicked,' he says at one point, and 'Why should I bother?' at another."

"It sounds interesting. But he goes on bothering?"

"Yes, that's the incredible thing."

Tea arrived, the young nurse handing Gill her cup. There was a plate of biscuits for them.

"I've brought you some letters from the flat, and here's your key." She held the small Yale key towards him, but he shook his head.

"Keep it," he said, "please. I've got a spare one."

They studied one another.

"All right," Gill said finally. "I will. Thanks." With that, she handed him the three letters. He sorted through them in a second.

"He's started sending them by mail, I see." Rebus tore open the latest bulletin. "This guy," he said, "is haunting me. Mister Knot, I call him. My own personal anonymous crank."

Gill looked interested, as Rebus read through the letter. It was longer than usual.

YOU STILL HAVEN'T GUESSED, HAVE YOU? YOU'VE NO IDEAS. NOT AN IDEA IN YOUR HEAD. AND IT'S ALMOST OVER NOW, ALMOST OVER. DON'T SAY I'VE NOT GIVEN YOU A CHANCE. YOU CAN NEVER SAY THAT. SIGNED

Rebus pulled a small matchstick cross out of the envelope.

"Ah, Mister Cross today, I see. Well, thank God he's nearly finished. Getting bored, I suppose."

"What is all this, John?"

"Haven't I told you about my anonymous letters? It's not a very exciting story."

"How long has this been going on?" Gill, having studied the letter, was now examining the envelope.

"Six weeks. Maybe a little longer. Why?"

"Well, it's just that this letter was posted on the day Helen Abbot went missing."

"Oh?" Rebus reached for the envelope and looked at its postmark. "Borders" it said. Rebus remembered that the others had been postmarked variously "Edinburgh," "Lothian," "Fife." A big enough area. He thought again of Michael.

"I don't suppose you can remember when you received the other letters?"

"What are you getting at, Gill?" He looked up at her, and saw a professional policewoman suddenly staring back at him. "For Christ's sake, Gill. This case is getting to all of us. We're all beginning to see ghosts."

"I'm just curious, that's all." She was reading the letter again. It was not the usual crank's voice, nor a crank's style. That was what worried her. And now that Rebus thought about it, the notes had seemed to appear around the time of each abduction, hadn't they? Had there been a connection of some kind staring him in the face all this time? He had been very myopic indeed, had been wearing a cart-horse's blinkers. Either that or it was all a monstrous coincidence.

"It's just a coincidence, Gill."

"So tell me when the other notes arrived."

"I can't remember."

She bent over him, her eyes huge behind her glasses. She said calmly, "Are you hiding anything from me?"

"No!"

The whole ward turned to his cry, and he felt his cheeks flush.

"No," he whispered, "I'm not hiding anything. At least
. . ." But how could he be sure? All those years of arrests, of
charge-sheets, of forgettings, so many enemies made. But
none would torment him like this, surely. Surely.

With pen, paper, and a lot of thought on his part, they went
over the arrival of each note: dates, contents, style of delivery.
Gill took off her glasses, rubbing between her eyes, sighing.

"It's just too big a coincidence, John."

And he knew that she was right, way down inside him. He
knew that nothing was ever what it seemed, that nothing was
arbitrary. "Gill," he said at last, pulling at the bedcover, "I've
got to get out of here."

In the car she goaded him, spurred him on. Who could it be?
What was the connection? Why?

"What is this?" he roared at her. "Am I a suspect now or
something?"

She studied his eyes, trying to pierce them, trying to bite
right into the truth behind them. Oh, she was a detective at
heart, and a good detective trusts nobody. She gazed at him as
though he were a scolded schoolboy, with secrets still to spill,
with sins to confess. Confess.

Gill knew that all this was only a hunch, insupportable. Yet
she could feel something there, something perhaps behind
those burning eyes. Stranger things had happened during her
time on the force. Strange things were always happening.
Truth was always stranger than fiction, and nobody was ever
wholly innocent. Those guilty looks when you questioned
somebody, anybody. Everyone had something to hide.
Mostly, though, it was small time, and covered by the years
intervening. You would need Thought Police to get at those
kinds of crime. But if John . . . If John Rebus proved to be
part of this whole caboodle, then that . . . That was too absurd to think about.

"Of course you're not a suspect, John," she said. "But it
could be important, couldn't it?"

"We'll let Anderson decide," he said, falling silent, but shaking.

It was then that Gill had the thought: what if he sent the letters to himself?

## XVIII

He felt his arms ache and, looking down, saw that the girl had stopped struggling. There came that point, that sudden, blissful point, when it was useless to go on living, and when the mind and body came to accept that such was the case. That was a beautiful, peaceful moment, the most relaxed moment of one's life. He had, many years ago, tried to commit suicide, savouring that very moment. But they had done things to him in hospital and in the clinic afterwards. They had given him back the will to live, and now he was repaying them, repaying all of them. He saw this irony in his life and chuckled, peeling the tape from Helen Abbot's mouth, using the little scissors to snip away her bonds. He brought out a neat little camera from his trouser pocket and took another instant snap of her, a *memento mori* of sorts. If they ever caught him, they'd kick the shit out of him for this, but they would never be able to brand him a sex-killer. Sex had nothing to do with it; these girls were pawns, fated by their christenings. The next and last one was the one that really mattered, and he would do that one today if possible. He chuckled again. This was a better game than noughts and crosses. He was a winner at both.

## XIX

Chief Inspector William Anderson loved the feel of the chase, the battle between instinct and plodding detection. He liked to feel, too, that he had the support of his Division behind him. Dispenser of orders, of wisdom, of strategies, he was in his element.

He would rather have caught the Strangler already—that went without saying. He was no sadist. The law had to be upheld. All the same, the longer an investigation like this went on, the greater became the feel of nearing the kill, and to relish that extended moment was one of the great perks of responsibility.

The Strangler was making an occasional slip, and that was what mattered to Anderson at this stage. The blue Ford Escort, and now the interesting theory that the killer had been or was still an Army man, suggested by the tying of a knot in the garotte. Snippets like that would culminate eventually in a name, an address, an arrest. And at that moment, Anderson would lead his officers physically as well as spiritually. There would be another interview on the television, another rather flattering photograph in the press (he was quite photogenic). Oh yes, victory would be sweet. Unless, of course, the Strangler vanished in the night as so many before him had done. That possibility was not to be considered; it made his legs turn into paper.

He did not dislike Rebus, not exactly. The man was a reasonable enough copper, a bit loud in his methods perhaps. And he understood that Rebus's personal life had experienced an upheaval. Indeed, he had been told that Rebus's ex-wife was the woman with whom his son was co-habiting. He tried not to think about it. When Andy had slammed the front door on his leaving, he had walked right out of his father's life. How could anyone these days spend their time writing poetry? It was ludicrous. And then moving in with Rebus's wife . . . No, he did not dislike Rebus, but watching Rebus come towards him with that pretty Liaison Officer, Anderson felt his stomach cough, as though his insides suddenly wanted to become his outsides. He leaned back on the edge of a vacant desk. The officer assigned to it had gone off for a break.

"Nice to have you back, John. Feeling fit?"

Anderson had shot out his hand, and Rebus, stunned, was forced to take it and return the grip.

"I'm fine, sir," he said.

"Sir," interrupted Gill Templer, "can we speak to you for a minute? There's been a new development."

"The mere *hint* of a development, sir," corrected Rebus, staring at Gill.

Anderson looked from one to the other.

"You'd better come into my office then."

Gill explained the situation as she saw it to Anderson, and he, wise and safe behind his desk, listened, glancing occasionally towards Rebus, who smiled apologetically at him. Sorry to be wasting your time, Rebus's smile said.

"Well, Rebus?" said Anderson when Gill had finished. "What do you say to all this? Could someone have a reason for informing you of their plans? I mean, could the Strangler *know* you?"

Rebus shrugged his shoulders, smiling, smiling, smiling.

Jack Morton, sitting in his car, jotted down some remarks on his report-sheet. Saw suspect. Interviewed same. Casual, helpful. Another dead end, he wanted to say. Another dead fucking end. A parking warden was looking at him, trying to scare him as she neared his car. He sighed, putting down the pen and paper and reaching for his I.D. One of those days.

Rhona Phillips wore her raincoat, it being the end of May, and the rain slashing through the skyline as though painted upon an artist's canvas. She kissed her curly-headed poet-lover good-bye, as he watched afternoon TV, and left the house, feeling for the car-keys in her handbag. She picked Sammy up from school these days, though the school was only a mile and a quarter away. She also went with her to the library at lunch-times, not allowing her any escape. With that maniac still on the loose, she was taking no chances. She rushed to her car, got in, and slammed shut the door. Edinburgh rain was like a judgement. It soaked into the bones, into the structures of the buildings, into the memories of the tourists. It lingered for days, splashing up from puddles by the roadside, breaking up marriages, chilling, killing, omnipresent. The typical postcard home from an Edinburgh boarding-house: "Edinburgh is lovely. The people rather reserved. Saw the Castle yesterday, and the Scott Monument. It's a very small city, almost a town really. You could fit it inside New York and never notice it. Weather could be better."

Weather could be better. The art of euphemism. Shitty, shitty rain. It was so typical when she had a free day. Typical, too, that Andy and she should have argued. And now he was sulking in his chair, legs tucked beneath him. One of those days. And she had reports to write out this evening. Thank God the exams had started. The kids seemed more subdued at school these days, the older ones gripped by exam-fever or exam-apathy, and the younger ones seeing their ineluctable future mapped out for them in the faces of their doomed superiors. It was an interesting time of year. Soon the fear would be Sammy's, called Samantha to her face now that she was so nearly a woman. There were other fears there, too, for a parent. The fear of adolescence, of experiment.

As she reversed the car out of the driveway, he watched her from his Escort. Perfect. He had about fifteen minutes to wait. When her car had disappeared, he drove his car to the front of the house and stopped. He examined the windows of the house. Her man would be in there alone. He left his car and walked to the front door.

Back in the Incident Room after the inconclusive meeting, Rebus could not know that Anderson was arranging to have him put under surveillance. The Incident Room looked like an incident itself. Paper covered every surface, a small computer was crammed into a spare corner, charts and rotas and the rest covered every available inch of wall-space.

"I've got a briefing," said Gill. "I'll see you later. Listen,

John, I do think there's a link. Call it female intuition, call it a detective's "nose," call it what you like, but take me seriously. Think it over. Think about possible grudges. Please."

He nodded, then watched her leave, making for her own office in her own part of the building. Rebus wasn't sure which desk was his any more. He surveyed the room. It all seemed different somehow, as though a few of the desks had been changed around or put together. A telephone rang on the desk next to him. And though there were officers and telephonists nearby, he picked it up himself, making an attempt to get back into the investigation. He prayed that he was not himself the investigation. He prayed, forgetting what prayer was.

"Incident Room," he said. "Detective Sergeant Rebus speaking."

"Rebus? What a curious name that is." The voice was old but lively, certainly well-educated. "Rebus," it said again, as though jotting it down onto a piece of paper. Rebus studied the telephone.

"And your name, sir?"

"Oh, I'm Michael Eiser, that's E-I-S-E-R, Professor of English Literature at the University."

"Oh, yes, sir?" Rebus grabbed a pencil and jotted down the name. "And what can I do for you, sir?"

"Well, Mister Rebus, it's more a case of what I *think* I can do for you, though of course I may be mistaken." Rebus had a picture of the man, if this were not a hoax call: frizzy-haired, bow-tied, wearing crushed tweeds and old shoes, and waving his hands about as he spoke. "I'm interested in word-play, you see. In fact, I'm writing a book on the subject. It's called *Reading Exercises and Directed Exegetic Responses.* Do you see the word-play there? It's an acrostic. The first letter of each word makes up another word—*reader,* in this case. It's a game as old as literature itself. My book, however, concentrates on its manifestation in more recent works. Nabokov and Burgess and the like. Of course, acrostics are a small part of the over-all set of ploys used by the author to entertain, direct, or persuade his audience." Rebus tried to interrupt the man, but it was like trying to interrupt a bull. So he was forced to listen, wondering all the time if it were a crank call, if he should—strictly against procedure—simply put down the telephone. He had more important things to think about. The back of his head ached.

". . . and the point is, Mister Rebus, that I have noticed, quite by chance, a kind of pattern in this murderer's choice of victims."

Rebus sat down on the edge of the desk. He clasped the pencil as though trying to crush it.

"Oh, yes?" he said.

"Yes. I have the names of the victims here in front of me on a piece of paper. Perhaps one would have noticed it sooner, but it was only today that I saw a report in one newspaper which grouped the poor girls together. I usually take *The Times,* you see, but I quite simply couldn't find one this morning, so I bought another paper, and there it was. It may be nothing at all, mere coincidence, but then again it may not. I'll leave that for you chaps to decide. I merely offer it as a proposition."

Jack Morton, puffing smoke all around him, entered the office and, noticing Rebus, waved. Rebus jerked his head in response. Jack looked worn out. Everyone looked worn out, and here he was, fresh from a period of rest and relaxation, dealing with a lunatic on the telephone.

"Offer what exactly, Professor Eiser?"

"Well, don't you see? In order, the victims names were Sandra Adams, Mary Andrews, Nicola Turner, and Helen Abbot." Jack slouched towards Rebus's table. "Taken as an acrostic," continued the voice, "their names make up another name—Samantha. The murderer's next victim, perhaps? Or it may be simple coincidence, a game where no game really exists."

Rebus slammed down the telephone, was off the desk in a second, and pulled Jack Morton around by his neck-tie. Morton gasped and his cigarette flew from his mouth.

"Got your car outside, Jack?"

Still choking, he nodded a reply.

Jesus Christ, Jesus Christ. It was all true then. It was all to do with *him*. Samantha. All the clues, all the killings had been meant merely as a message to *him*. Jesus Christ. Help me, oh help me.

His daughter was to be the strangler's next victim.

Rhona Phillips saw the car parked outside her house, but thought nothing of it. All she wanted was to get out of the rain. She ran to the front door, Samantha following desultorily behind, and keyed open the door.

"It's horrible outside!" she shouted into the living-room. She shook off her raincoat and walked through to where the TV still blared. In his chair, she saw Andy. His hands were tied behind him and his mouth was taped shut with a huge piece of sticking-plaster. The length of twine still dangled from his throat.

Rhona was about to let out the most piercing scream of her life, when a heavy object came down on the back of her head and she staggered forward towards her lover, slumping across his legs as she passed out.

"Hello, Samantha," said a voice she recognised, though his face was masked so that she could not see his smile.

Morton's car tore across town, its blue light flashing, as though it were being followed by all Hell itself. Rebus tried explaining it all as they drove, but he was too edgy to make much sense, and Jack Morton was too busy avoiding traffic to make much attempt at taking it in. They had called for assistance: one car to the school in case she were still there, and two cars to the house, with the warning that the Strangler might be there. Caution was to be exercised.

The car reached eighty-five along Queensferry Road, made an insane right turn across the oncoming traffic, and reached the bright-as-a-pin housing estate where Rhona, Samantha, and Rhona's lover now lived.

"Turn right here," shouted Rebus over the engine's roar, his mind clinging to hope. As they turned into the street they saw the two police cars already motionless in front of the house, and Rhona's car sitting like a potent symbol of futility in the driveway.

## XX

They wanted to give him sedatives, but he wouldn't take any of their drugs. They wanted him to go home, but he would not take their advice. How could he go home with Rhona lying somewhere above him in the hospital? With his daughter abducted, his whole life ripped apart like a worn garment being transformed into dusters? He paced the hospital waiting-room. He was fine, he told them, fine. He knew that Gill and Anderson were somewhere along the corridor. Poor Anderson. He watched from the grime of the window as nurses walked by outside, laughing in the rain, their capes blowing about them like something out of an old Dracula movie. How could they laugh? Mist was settling over the trees, and the nurses, still laughing, unaware of the world's suffering, faded into that mist as though some Edinburgh of the past had sucked them into its fiction, taking with them all the laughter in the world.

It was nearly dark now, the sun a memory behind the heavy fabric of the clouds. The religious painters of old must have known skies like this, must have lived with them each and every day, accepting the bruised colouring of the clouds as a mark of God's presence, an essence of creation's power. Rebus was no painter. His eyes beheld beauty not in reality but in the printed word. Standing in the waiting-room, he realised that in his life he had accepted secondary experience— the experience of reading someone else's thoughts—over real life. Well, he was face to face with it now all right: he was back in the Paras, he was back in the SAS, his face a sketch-pad of exhaustion, his brain aching, every muscle tensed.

He caught himself beginning to abstract everything again, and slapped the wall with the palms of both hands as though ready to be frisked. Sammy was out there somewhere in the hands of a maniac, and he was composing eulogies, excuses, and similes. It wasn't enough.

In the corridor, Gill kept a watch on William Anderson. He, too, had been told to go home. A doctor had examined him for the effects of shock, and had spoken of putting Anderson to bed for the night.

"I'm waiting right here," Anderson had said with quiet determination. "If this all has something to do with John Rebus, then I want to stay close to John Rebus. I'm all right, honestly." But he was not all right. He was dazed and remorseful and a bit confused about everything. "I can't believe it," he told Gill. "I can't believe that this whole thing was merely a prelude to the abduction of Rebus's daughter. It's fantastical. The man must be deranged. Surely John must have an inkling who's responsible?"

Gill Templer was wondering the same thing.

"Why hasn't he told us?" continued Anderson. Then, without warning or any show of ceremony, he became a father again and started to sob very quietly. "Andy," he said, "my Andy." He put his head in his hands and allowed Gill to put her arm around his crumpled shoulders.

John Rebus, watching darkness descend, thought about his marriage, his daughter. His daughter Sammy.

*For those who read between the times*

What was it he was blocking out? What was it that had been rejected by him all those years ago as he had walked the Fife shoreline, having his final fit of the breakdown and shutting out the past as securely as if he had been shutting the door on a Jehovah's Witness? It was not that easy. The unwanted caller had waited his time, deciding to break and enter into Rebus's life again. The foot in the door. The door of perception. What good was his reding doing him now? Or his faith, slender thread that it was? Samantha. Sammy, his daughter. Dear God, let her be safe. Dear God, let her live.

*John, you must know who it is*

But he had shaken his head, shaken his tears onto the folds of his trousers. He did not, he did not. It was Knot. It was Cross. Names meant nothing to him any more. Knots and crosses. He had been sent knots and crosses, string and matches and a load of gobbledygook, as Jack Morton had called it. That was all. Dear God.

He went out into the corridor, and confronted Anderson, who stood before him like a piece of wreckage waiting to be loaded up and shunted away. And the two men came together in a hug, squeezing life into one another; two old enemies realising in a moment that they were on the same side after all. They hugged and they wept, draining themselves of all they had been bottling up, all those years of pounding the beat, having to appear emotionless and unflappable. It was out in the open now: they were human beings, the same as everybody else.

And finally, assured that Rhona had suffered a fractured skull only, allowed into her room for a moment to watch her breathing oxygen, Rebus had let them take him home. Rhona would live. That was something. Andy Anderson, though, was cold on a slab somewhere while doctors examined his leftovers. Poor bloody Anderson. Poor man, poor father, poor copper. It was becoming very personal now, wasn't it? All of a sudden it had become bigger than they had imagined it ever could. It had become a grudge.

They had a description at last, though not a good one. A neighbour had seen the man carry the still form of the girl out to the car. A pale coloured car, she had told them. A normal looking car. A normal looking man. Not too tall, his face hard. He was hurrying. She didn't get a good look at him.

Anderson would be off the case now, and so would Rebus. Oh, it was big now. The Strangler had entered a home, had murdered there. He had gone way too far over the edge. The newspapermen and the cameras outside the hospital wanted to know all about it. Superintendent Wallace would have organised a press conference. The newspaper-readers, the voyeurs needed to know all about it. It was big news. Edinburgh was the crime capital of Europe. The son of a Chief Inspector murdered and the daughter of a Detective Sergeant abducted, possibly murdered already.

What could he do but sit and wait for another letter? He was better off in his flat, no matter how dark and barren it seemed, no matter how like a cell. Gill promised to visit him later, after the press conference. An unmarked car would be outside his tenement as a matter of course, for who knew how personal the Strangler wanted this to become?

Meantime, unknown to Rebus, his file was being checked back at HQ, his past dusted off and examined. There had to be the Strangler in there somewhere. There had to be.

Of course there had to be. Rebus knew that he alone held the key. But it seemed locked in a drawer to which it itself was the key. He could only rattle that locked-away history.

Gill Templer had telephoned Rebus's brother, and though John would hate her for doing so, she had told Michael to come across to Edinburgh at once to be with his brother. He was Rebus's only family after all. He sounded nervous on the phone, nervous but concerned. And now she puzzled over the matter of the acrostic. The Professor had been correct. They were trying to locate him this evening in order to interview him. Again, as a matter of course. But if the Strangler had planned this, then surely he must have been able to get his hands on a list of people whose names would fit the bill, and how would he have done that? A civil servant perhaps? A teacher? Someone working away quietly at a computer-terminal somewhere? There were many possibilities, and they would go through them one by one. First, however, Gill was going to suggest that everyone in Edinburgh called Knott be interviewed. It was a wild card, but then everything about this case so far had been wild.

And then there was the press conference. Held, since it was convenient, in the hospital's administration building. There was standing room only at the back of the hall. Gill Templer's face, human but unsmiling, was becoming well known to the British public, as well known, certainly, as that of any newscaster or reporter. Tonight, however, the Superintendent would be doing the talking. She hoped he would not take long. She wanted to see Rebus. And more urgently, perhaps, she wanted to talk with his brother. Someone had to know about John's past. He had never, apparently, spoken to any of his friends on the force about his Army years. Did the key lie there? Or in his marriage? Gill listened to the Super saying his piece. Cameras clicked and the large hall grew smoky.

And there was Jim Stevens, smiling from the corner of his mouth, as if he knew something. Gill grew nervous. His eyes were on her, though his pen worked away at its notepad. She recalled that disastrous evening they had spent together, and her much less disastrous evening with John Rebus. Why had none of the men in her life ever been uncomplicated? Perhaps because complications interested her. The case was not becoming more complex. It was becoming simpler.

Jim Stevens, half-listening to the police statement, thought of how complex this story was becoming. Rebus and Rebus, drugs and murder, anonymous messages followed by abduction of daughter. He needed to get behind the police's public face on this one, and knew that the best way forward lay with Gill Templer, with a little trading of knowledge. If the drugs and the abduction were linked, as they probably were, then perhaps one or other of the Rebus brothers had not been playing the game according to the set rules. Maybe Gill Templer would know.

He came up behind her as she left the buildings. She knew it was him, but for once she wanted to speak with him.

"Hello, Jim. Can I give you a lift somewhere?"

He decided that she could. She could drop him off at a bar, unless, of course, he could see Rebus for a moment? He could not. They drove.

"This story is becoming more and more bizarre by the second, don't you think?"

She concentrated her eyes on the road, seeming to mull over his question. Really, she was hoping he would open up a little more and that her silence would lead him to believe that she was holding back on him, that there was something there between them to swap.

"Rebus seemed to be the main actor, though. Interesting that."

Gill sensed that he was about to play a card.

"I mean," he went on, lighting a cigarette, "don't mind if I smoke, do you?"

"No," she said slowly, though inside she was jarring with electricity.

"Thanks. I mean, it's interesting because I've got Rebus pencilled into another story I'm working on."

She pulled the car up at a red light, but her eyes still gazed through the windscreen.

"Would you be interested in hearing about this other story, Gill?"

Would she? Of course she would. But what in return . . .

"Yes, a very interesting man, Mr. Rebus. And his brother."

"His brother?"

"Yes, you know, Michael Rebus, the hypnotist. An interesting pair of brothers."

"Oh?"

"Listen, Gill, let's cut the crap."

"I was hoping you would." She put the car into gear and started off again.

"Are you lot investigating Rebus for anything? that's what I want to know. I mean, do you really know who's behind all this but aren't saying?"

She turned to him now.

"That's not the way it works, Jim."

He snorted.

"It may not be the way you work, Gill, but don't pretend it doesn't happen. I just wondered if you'd heard anything, any

rumbles from higher up. Maybe to the effect that someone
had made a botch-up in allowing things to come to this."

Jim Stevens was watching her face very closely indeed,
throwing out ideas and vague theories in the hope that one of
them would catch her. But she didn't seem to be taking the
bait. Very well. Maybe she didn't know anything. That didn't
mean his theories were wrong necessarily. It could just mean
that things started at a higher plane than that on which Gill
Templer and he operated.

"Jim, what is it you *think* you know about John Rebus. It
could be important, you know. We could bring you in if we
thought you were withholding . . ."

Stevens began to make tutting sounds, shaking his head.

"We know that's not on, don't we though? I mean, that is
just not on."

She looked at him again.

"I could make a precedent," she said.

He stared at her. Yes, maybe she could at that.

"This'll do just here," he said, pointing out of the window.
Some ash fell from his cigarette onto his tie. Gill stopped the
car and watched him climb out. He leaned back in before
shutting the door.

"A swap can be arranged if you'd like one. You know my
phone number."

Yes, she knew his phone number. He had written it down
for her a very long time ago, so long ago that they were on
different sides of a wall now, so that she could hardly understand him at all. What did he know about John? About Michael? As she drove off towards Rebus's flat, she hoped that
she would find out there.


## XXI

John Rebus read a few pages from his *Good News Bible,* but
put it down when he realised that he was taking none of it in.
He prayed instead, screwing up his eyes into tiny fists. Then

he walked around the flat, touching things. This he had done before that first breakdown. He was not afraid now, though. Let it come if it would, let everything come. He had no resilience left. He was passive to the will of his malevolent creator.

There was a ring at the door. He did not answer. They would go away, and he would be alone again with his grief, his impotent anger, and his undusted possessions. The bell rang again, more persistently this time. Cursing, he went to the door and pulled it open. Michael was standing there.

"John," he said, "I came as soon as I could."

"Mickey, what are you doing here?" He ushered his brother into the flat.

"Somebody phoned me. She told me all about it. Terrible news, John. Just terrible." He placed a hand on Rebus's shoulder. Rebus, tingling, realised how long it had been since he had felt the touch of a human being, a sympathetic, brotherly touch. "I was confronted by two gorillas outside. They seem to have you under close watch here."

"Procedure," said Rebus.

Procedure maybe, but Michael knew how guilty he must have looked when they had pounced on him. He had wondered at the phone-call, wondered about the possibility of a trap. So he had listened to the local radio news. There had been an abduction, a killing. It was true. So he had driven over, into this lion's den, knowing that he should stay well away from his brother, knowing that they would kill him if they found out, and wondering whether the abduction could have anything to do with his own situation. Was this a warning to both brothers? He could not say. But when those two gorillas had approached him in the shadows of the tenement stairs, he had thought it all over. Firstly, they had been gangsters, out to get him. Then, they had been police officers, about to arrest him. But no, they were "procedure."

"You say it was a woman who called you? Did you catch her name? No, never mind, I know who it was anyway."

They sat in the living-room. Michael, removing his sheepskin jacket, brought a bottle of whisky out of one of the pockets.

"Would this help?" he said.

"It won't do any harm."

Rebus went to fetch glasses from the kitchen, while Michael inspected the living-room.

"This is a nice place," he called.

"Well, it's a bit big for my needs," said Rebus. A choking sound came from the kitchen. Michael walked through to discover his big brother leaning into the sink, weeping grimly but quietly.

"John," said Michael, hugging Rebus, "it's okay. It's going to be okay." He felt guilt well up inside him.

Rebus was fumbling for a handkerchief and, having found it, gave his nose a good blow and wiped his eyes.

"That's easy for you to say," he sniffed, trying out a smile, "you're a heathen."

They drank half of the whisky, sitting back in their chairs, silently contemplating the shadowy ceiling above. Rebus's eyes were red-rimmed, and his eye-lashes stung. He sniffed occasionally, rubbing at his nose with the back of his hand. To Michael, it was like being boys again, but with the roles reversed for a moment. Not that they had been that close, but sentiment always would win over reality. Certainly he remembered John fighting one or two of his playground battles for him. Guilt welled up again. He shivered slightly. He had to get out of this game, but perhaps already he was in too deep, and if he had brought John unknowingly into the game, too . . . That did not bear thinking about. He had to see the Man, had to explain things to him. But how? He had no telephone number or address. It was always the Man who called him, never the other way round. It was farcical now that he thought about it. Like a nightmare.

"Did you enjoy the show the other night?"

Rebus forced himself to think back to it, to the perfumed

and lonely woman, to his fingers around her throat, the scene which had signalled the beginning of his end.

"Yes, it was interesting." He had fallen asleep, had he not? Never mind.

Silence again, the broken sounds of traffic outside, a few shouts from distant drunks.

"They say it's someone with a grudge against me," he said finally.

"Oh? And is it?"

"I don't know. It looks like it."

"But surely you would *know?*"

Rebus shook his head.

"That's the trouble, Mickey. I can't remember."

Michael sat up in his chair.

"You can't remember what, exactly?"

"Something. I don't know. Just something. If I knew what, I *would* remember, wouldn't I? But there's a gap. I know there is. I know that there's something I should remember."

"Something from your past?" Michael was keening now. Perhaps this had nothing at all to do with himself. Perhaps it was all to do with something else, someone else. He grew hopeful.

"From the past, yes. But I can't remember." Rebus rubbed his forehead as though it were a crystal ball. Michael was fumbling in his pocket.

"I can help you to remember, John."

"How?"

"Like this." Michael was holding, between thumb and fore-finger, a silver coin. "You remember what I told you, John. I take my patients back into past lives every day. It should be easy enough to take you back into your *real* past."

It was John Rebus's turn to sit up. He shook away the whisky fumes.

"Come on then," he said. "What do I do?" But inside part of him was saying: *you don't want this, you don't want to know.*

He wanted to know.

Michael came over to his chair.

"Lie back in the chair. Get comfortable. Don't touch any more of that whisky. But remember, not everyone is susceptible to hypnotism. Don't force yourself. Don't try too hard. If it's going to come, it'll come whether you will it or not. Just relax, John, relax."

The doorbell rang.

"Ignore it," said Rebus, but Michael had already left the room. There were voices in the hall, and when Michael reappeared he was followed into the room by Gill.

"The telephone caller, it seems," said Michael.

"How are you, John?" Her face was angled into a portrait of concern.

"Fine, Gill. Listen, this is my brother Michael. The hypnotist. He's going to put me under—that's what you called it, wasn't it, Mickey?—to remove whatever block there might be in my memory. Maybe you should be ready to take some notes or something."

Gill looked from one brother to the other, feeling a little out of things. An interesting pair of brothers. That's what Jim Stevens had said. She had been working for sixteen hours, and now this. But she smiled and shrugged her shoulders.

"Can a girl get a drink first?"

It was John Rebus's turn to smile. "Help yourself," he said. "There's whisky or whisky and water or water. Come on, Mickey. Let's get on with this. Sammy's out there somewhere. There might still be time."

Michael spread his legs a little, leaning down over Rebus. He seemed to be about to consume his brother, his eyes close to Rebus's eyes, his mouth working in a mirror-image. That's what it looked like to Gill, pouring whisky into a tumbler. Michael held up the coin, trying to find the angle of the room's single low-wattage bulb. Finally, the glint was reflected in John's retina, the pupils expanding and contracting. Michael felt sure that his brother would be amenable. He certainly hoped so.

"Listen carefully, John. Listen to my voice. Watch the coin, John. Watch it shine and spin. See it spinning. Can you see it spinning, John? Now relax, just listen to me. And watch the spin, watch it glow."

For a moment it seemed that Rebus would not go under. Perhaps it was the familial tie that was making him immune to the voice, to its suggestive power. But then Michael saw the eyes change a little, imperceptibly to the uninitiated. But he was initiated. His father had taught him well. His brother was in the limbo world now, caught in the coin's light, transported to wherever Michael wanted him to go. Under his power. As ever, Michael felt a little shiver run through him: this was power, power total and irreducible. He could do anything with his patients, anything.

"Michael," whispered Gill, "ask him why he left the Army."

Michael swallowed, lining his throat with saliva. Yes, that was a good question. One he had wanted to ask John himself.

"John?" he said. "John? Why did you leave the Army, John? What happened, John? Why did you leave the Army? Tell us."

And slowly, as though learning to use words strange or unknown to him, Rebus began to tell his story. Gill rushed to her bag for a pen and a notepad. Michael sipped his whisky.

They listened.

# PART FOUR

## *The Cross*

### XXII

I had been in the Parachute Regiment since the age of eighteen. But then I decided to try for the Special Air Service. Why did I do that? Why will any soldier take a cut in pay to join the SAS? I can't answer that. All I know now is that I found myself in Herefordshire, at the SAS's training camp. I called it The Cross because I'd been told that they would try to crucify me, and there, along with the other volunteers, I went through hell, marching, training, testing, pushing. They took us to the breaking point. They taught us to be lethal.

At that time there were rumours of an imminent civil war in Ulster, of the SAS being used to root out insurrectionists. The day came for us to be badged. We were given new berets and cap-badges. We were in the SAS. But there was more. Gordon Reeve and myself were called into the Boss's office and told that we had been judged the two best trainees of the batch. There was a two-year training period in front of us before we could become regulars, but great things were predicted for us.

Later, Reeve spoke to me as we left the building.

"Listen," he said, "I've heard a few rumours. I've heard the officers talking. They've got plans for us, Johnny. *Plans.* Mark my words."

Weeks later, we were put on a survival course, hunted by other regiments, who if they captured us would stop at noth-

ing to prise from us information about our mission. We had to
trap and hunt our food, lying low and travelling across bleak
moorland by night. We seemed destined to go through these
tests together, though on this occasion we were working with
two others.

"They've got something special lined up for us," Reeve
kept saying. "I can feel it in my bones."

Lying in our bivouac, we had just slipped into our sleeping-
bags for the two-hour nap when our guard put his nose into
the shelter.

"I don't know how to tell you this," he said, and then there
were lights and guns everywhere, and we were half-beaten
into consciousness as the shelter was ripped open. Foreign
tongues clacked at us, their faces masked behind the torches.
A rifle-butt to the kidneys told me that this was for real. *For
real.*

The cell into which I was thrown was real enough, too. The
cell into which I was thrown was smeared with blood, faeces,
and other things. It contained a stinking mattress and a cockroach. That was all. I lay down on the damp mattress and tried
to sleep, for I knew that sleep would be the first thing to be
stripped from us all.

The bright lights of the cell came on suddenly and stayed
on, burning into my skull. Then the noises started, noises of a
beating and a questioning taking place in the cell next to me.

"Leave him alone, you bastards! I'll tear your sodding heads
off!"

I slammed at the wall with fists and boots, and the noises
stopped. A cell door slammed shut, a body was dragged past
my metal door, there was silence. I knew my time would
come.

I waited there, waited for hours and days, hungry, thirsty,
and every time I closed my eyes a sound like that of a blaring
radio caught between stations would sound from the walls
and the ceiling. I lay with my hands over my ears.

I was supposed to crack now, and if I cracked I would have
failed everything, all the months of training. So I sang tunes

loudly to myself. I scraped my nails across the walls of the cell, walls wet with fungus, and scratched my name there as an anagram: BRUSE. I played games in my head, thought up crossword-puzzle clues and little linguistic tricks. I turned survival into a game. A game, a game, a game. I had to keep reminding myself that, no matter how bad things seemed to be getting, this was all a game.

And I thought of Reeve, who had warned me of this. Big plans indeed. Reeve was the nearest thing I had to a friend in the unit. I wondered if it had been his body dragged across the floor outside my cell. I prayed for him.

And one day they sent me food and a mug of brown water. The food looked as though it had been scooped straight from the mud-crawl and pushed through the little hole which had suddenly appeared in my door and just as suddenly vanished. I willed this cold swill into becoming a steak with two veg, and then placed a spoonful of it in my mouth. Immediately, I spat it out again. The water tasted of iron. I made a show of wiping my chin on my sleeve. I felt sure I was being watched.

"My compliments to the chef," I called.

Next thing I knew, I was falling over into sleep.

I was in the air. There could be no doubt of that. I was in a helicopter, the air blowing into my face. I came round slowly, and opened my eyes on darkness. My head was in some kind of sack, and my arms were tied behind my back. I felt the helicopter swoop and rise and swoop again.

"Awake, are you?" A butt prodded me.

"Yes."

"Good. Now give me the name of your regiment and the details of your mission. We're not going to mess around with you, sonny. So you better do it now."

"Get stuffed."

"I hope you can swim, sonny. I hope you get the *chance* to swim. We're about two-hundred feet above the Irish Sea, and we're about to push you out of this chopper with your hands still tied. You'll hit that water as though it was concrete, do you know that? It may kill you or it may stun you. The fish will eat you alive, sonny. And your corpse will never be found, not out here. Do you understand what I'm saying?"

It was an official and business-like voice.

"Yes."

"Good. Now, the name of your regiment, and the details of your mission."

"Get stuffed." I tried to sound calm. I'd be another accident statistic, killed on training, no questions asked. I'd hit the sea like a light-bulb hitting a wall.

"Get stuffed," I said again, intoning to myself: it's only a game, it's only a game.

"This isn't a game, you know. Not anymore. Your friends have already spilled their guts, Rebus. One of them, Reeve, I think it was, spilled his guts quite literally. Okay, men, give him the heave."

"Wait . . ."

"Enjoy your swim, Rebus."

Hands gripped my legs and torso. In the darkness of the sack, with the wind blowing fiercely against me, I began to feel that it had all been a grave mistake.

"Wait . . ."

I could feel myself hanging in space, two-hundred feet up above the sea, with the gulls shrieking for me to be let go.

"Wait!"

"Yes, Rebus?"

"Take the sack off my head at least!" I was shrieking now, desperate.

"Let the bastard drop."

And with that they let me go. I hung in the air for a second, then I dropped, dropped like a brick. I was falling through space, trussed up like a Christmas turkey. I screamed for one second, maybe two, and then I hit the ground.

*I hit solid ground.*

And lay there while the helicopter landed. People were laughing all around me. The foreign voices were back. They lifted me up and dragged me along to the cell. I was glad of the sack over my head. It disguised the fact that I was crying. Inside I was a mass of quivering coils, tiny serpents of fear and adrenalin and relief which bounced through my liver, my lungs, my heart.

The door slammed behind me. Then I heard a shuffling sound at my back. Hands fumbled at the knots of my bonds. With the hood off, it took me a few seconds to regain my sight.

I stared into a face that seemed to be my own. Another twist to the game. Then I recognised Gordon Reeve, at the same time as he recognised me.

"Rebus?" he said. "They told me you'd . . ."

"They told me the same thing about you. How are you?"

"Fine, fine. Jesus, though, I'm glad to see you."

We hugged one another, feeling the other's weakened but still human embrace, the smells of suffering and of endurance. There were tears in his eyes.

"It *is* you," he said. "I'm not dreaming."

"Let's sit down," I said. "My legs aren't too steady."

What I meant was that his legs weren't too steady. He was leaning into me as if I were a crutch. He sat down thankfully.

"How has it been?" I asked.

"I kept in shape for a while." He slapped one of his legs. "Doing push-ups and stuff. But I soon grew too tired. They've tried feeding me with hallucinogens. I keep seeing things when I'm awake."

"They've tried me with knockout drops."

"Those drugs, they're something else. Then there's the power-hose. I get sprayed about once a day, I suppose. Freezing cold. Can never seem to get dry."

"How long do you suppose we've been here?" Did I look as bad to him as he looked to me? I hoped not. He hadn't mentioned the chopper drop. I decided to keep quiet about that one.

"Too long," he was saying. "This is ridiculous."

"You were always saying that they had something special in store for us. I didn't believe you, God forgive me."

"This wasn't exactly what I had in mind."

"It *is* us they're interested in, though."

"What do you mean?"

It had been only half a thought until now, but now I was sure.

"Well, when our sentry put his nose into the tent that night, there was no surprise in his eyes, and even less fear. I think they were both in on it from the start."

"So what's this all about?"

I looked at him, sitting with his chin on his knees. We were frail creatures on the outside. Piles biting like the hungered jaws of vampire bats, mouths aching with sores and ulcers. Hair falling out, teeth loose. But there was strength in numbers. And that was what I could not understand: why had they put us together when, apart, we were both on the edge of breaking?

"So what's this all about?"

Perhaps they were trying to lull us into a false sense of security before really tightening the screws. The worst is not, so long as we can say "this is the worst." Shakespeare, *King Lear.* I wouldn't have known that at the time, but I know it now. Let it stand.

"I don't know," I said. "They'll tell us when they're good and ready, I suppose."

"Are you scared?" he said suddenly. His eyes were staring at the raddled door of our cell.

"Maybe."

"You should be scared, Johnny. I am. I remember once when I was a kid, some of us went along a river near our housing-scheme. It was in spate. It had been pissing down for a week. It was just after the war, and there were a lot of ruined houses about. We headed upriver, and came to a sewage-pipe. I played with older kids. I don't know why. They made me the brunt of all their games, but I stuck with them. I suppose I liked the idea of running about with kids who scared the shit out of all the kids of my own age. So that, though the older kids were treating me like shit, they gave me power over the younger kids. Do you see?"

I nodded, but he wasn't looking.

"This pipe wasn't very thick, but it was long, and it was high above the river. They said I was to cross it first. Christ, I was afraid. I was so scared that my legs wobbled and I froze there, halfway across. And then piss started to run down my legs out of my shorts, and they noticed that and they laughed. They laughed at me, and I couldn't run, couldn't move. So they left me there and went away."

I thought of the laughter as I had been dragged away from the helicopter.

"Did anything like that ever happen to you when you were a kid, Johnny?"

"I don't think so."

"Then why the hell did you join up?"

"To get away from home. I didn't get along with my father, you see. He preferred my kid brother. I felt out in the cold."

"I never had a brother."

"Neither did I, not in the proper sense. I had an adversary."

*I'm going to bring him out*
*don't you dare*
*This isn't telling us anything*
*keep going*

"What did your father do, Johnny?"

"He was a hypnotist. He used to make people come on stage and do stupid things."

"You're joking!"

"It's true. My brother was going to follow in his footsteps, but I wasn't. So I got out. They weren't exactly sad to see me go."

Reeve chuckled.

"If you put us into a sale, you'd have to say 'slightly soiled" on the ticket, eh, Johnny?"

I laughed at that, laughed longer and louder than necessary, and we put an arm round one another and stayed that way, keeping warm.

We slept side by side, pissed and shat in the presence of the other, tried to exercise together, played little mind games together, and endured together.

Reeve had a piece of string with him, and would wind it and unwind it, making up the knots we had been taught in training. This led me to explain the meaning of a Gordian knot to him. He waved a miniature reef knot at me.

"Gordian knot, reef knot. Gordian reef. It sounds just like my name, doesn't it?"

Again, there was something to laugh about.

We also played noughts and crosses, scratching the games onto the powdery walls of the cell with our fingernails. Reeve showed me a ploy which meant that the least you could achieve was a draw. We must have played about three-hundred games before then, with Reeve winning two-thirds of them. The trick was simple enough.

"Your first *O* goes in the top left corner, and your second diagonally across from it. It's an unbeatable position."

"What if your opponent puts his *X* diagonally opposite that first *O?*"

"You can still win by going for the corners."

Reeve seemed cheered by this. He danced round the cell, then stared at me, a leer on his face.

"You're just like the brother I never had, John." There and then he took my palm and nicked the flesh open with one of his fingernails, doing the same to his own hand. We touched palms, smearing a spot of blood backwards and forwards.

"Blood brothers," said Gordon, smiling.

I smiled back at him, knowing that he had become too dependent on me already, and that if we were separated he would not be able to cope.

And then he knelt down in front of me and gave me another hug.

Gordon grew more restless. He did fifty push-ups in any one day which, considering our diet, was phenomenal. And he hummed little tunes to himself. The effects of my company seemed to be wearing off. He was drifting again. So I began to tell him stories.

I talked about my childhood first, and about my father's tricks, but then I started to tell him proper stories, giving him the plots of my favourite books. The time came to tell him the story of Raskolnikov, that most moral of tales, *Crime and Punishment.* He listened enthralled, and I tried to spin it out as long as I could. I made bits up, invented whole dialogues and characters. And when I'd finished it, he said, "Tell me that one again."

So I did.

"Was it all inevitable, John?" Reeve was pushing his fingers across the floor of the cell, seated on his haunches. I was lying on the mattress.

"Yes," I said. "I think it was. Certainly, it's written that way. The end of the book is there before the beginning's hardly started."

"Yes, that's the feeling I got."

There was a long pause, then he cleared his throat.

"What's your idea of God, John. I'd really like to know."

So I told him, and as I spoke, lacing my erroneous arguments with little stories from the Bible, Gordon Reeve lay down and stared up at me with eyes like the full moons of winter. He was concentrating like mad.

"I can't belive any of that," he said at last as I swallowed dry saliva. "I wish I could, but I can't. I think Raskolnikov should have relaxed and enjoyed his freedom. He should have got himself a Browning and blown the lot of them away."

I thought about that comment. There seemed to me a little justice in it, but a great deal against it also. Reeve was like a man trapped in limbo, believing in a lack of belief, but not necessarily lacking the belief to believe.

*What's all this shit?*

*Sshhh*

And in between the games and the story-telling, he put his hand on my neck.

"John, we're friends, aren't we? I mean, really close

friends? I've never had a close friend before." His breath was hot, despite the chill in the cell. "But we're friends, aren't we? I mean, I've taught you how to win at noughts and crosses, haven't I?" His eyes were no longer human. They were the eyes of a wolf. I had seen it coming, but there had been nothing I could do.

Not until now. But now I saw everything with the clear, hallucinogen eyes of one who has seen everything there is to see and more. I could see Gordon bring his face up to mine and slowly—so slowly that it might not have been happening at all—plant a breathy kiss on my cheek, trying to turn my head around so as to connect with the lips.

And I saw myself yield. No, no, this was not to happen! This was intolerable. This wasn't what we'd been building up all these weeks, was it? And if it was, then I'd been a fool throughout.

"Just a kiss," he was saying, "just one kiss, John. Hell, come on." And there were tears in his eyes, because he too could see that everything had gone haywire in an instant. He too could see that something was ending. But that didn't stop him from edging his way behind me, making the two-backed beast. (Shakespeare. Let it go.) And I was trembling, but strangely immobile. I knew that this was beyond my ken, beyond my control. So I forced the tears up into my eyes, and my nose started to run.

"Just a kiss."

All the training, all the pushing towards that final lethal goal, it had all come to this moment. In the end, love was still behind everything.

"John."

And I could feel only pity for the two of us, stinking, besmirched, barren in our cell. I could feel only the frustration of the thing, the poor tears of a lifetime's indignation. Gordon, Gordon, Gordon.

"John . . ."

The cell-door burst open, as though it had never been locked.

A man stood there. English, not foreign, and of high rank. He looked in on the spectacle with some distaste; no doubt he had been listening to it all, if not watching it. He pointed to me.

"Rebus," he said, "you've passed. You're on our side now."

I looked at his face. What did he mean? I knew full well what he meant.

"You've passed the test, Rebus. Come on. Come with me. We'll get you kitted up. You're on our side now. The interrogation of your . . . friend . . . continues. You'll be helping us with the interrogation from now on."

Gordon jumped to his feet. He was directly behind me still. I could feel his breath on the back of my neck.

"What do you mean?" I said. My mouth and stomach were dry. Looking at this crisply starched officer, I became painfully aware of my own filth. But then it was all his fault. "This is a trick," I said. "It must be. I'm not going to tell you. I'm not going *with* you. I've not given away any information. I've not cracked. You can't fail me now!" I was shouting now, delirious. Yet I knew there was truth in what he was saying. He shook his head slowly.

"I can understand your suspicion, Rebus. You've been under a lot of pressure. A hellish lot of pressure. But that's past. You've not failed, you've passed; passed with flying colours. I think we can say that with certainty. You've passed, Rebus. You're on our side now. You'll be helping us now to try to crack Reeve here. Do you understand?"

I shook my head.

"It's a trick," I said. The officer smiled sympathetically. He'd dealt with the like of me a hundred times before.

"Look," he said, "just come with me and everything will be made clear."

Gordon jumped forward at my side.

"No!" he shouted. "He's already told you that he's not going! Now piss off out of here." Then to me, a hand on my shoulder: "Don't listen to him, John. It's a trick. It's always a trick with these bastards." But I could see that he was worried. His eyes moved rapidly, his mouth slightly open. And, feeling his hand on me, I knew that my decision had been made already, and Gordon seemed to sense as much.

"I think that's for Trooper Rebus to decide, don't you?" the officer was saying.

And then the man stared at me, his eyes friendly.

I didn't need to look back at the cell, or at Gordon. I just kept thinking to myself: it's another part of the game, just another part of the game. The decision had been made a long time ago. They were not lying to me, and of course I wanted out of the cell. It was preordained. Nothing was arbitrary. I had been told that at the start of my training. I started forwards, but Gordon held onto the tatters of my shirt.

"John," he said, his voice full of need, "don't let me down, John. Please."

But I pulled away from his weak grip and left the cell.

"No! No! No!" His cries were huge, fiery things. "Don't let me down, John! Let me out! Let me out!"

And then he screamed, and I almost crumpled on the floor. It was the scream of the mad.

After I had been cleaned up and seen by a doctor, I was taken to what they euphemistically called the debriefing-room. I'd been through hell—was still going through hell—and they were about to discuss it as though it had been nothing more than a school exercise.

There were four of them there, three captains and a psychiatrist. They told me everything then. They explained that a new, elitist group was about to be set up from within the SAS, and that its role would be the infiltration and destabilization of terrorist groups, starting with the Irish Republican Army, who were becoming more than a mere nuisance as the Irish situation deteriorated into civil war. Because of the nature of the job, only the best—the very best—would be good enough, and Reeve and I had been judged the best in our section. Therefore, we had been trapped, had been taken prisoner, and had been put through tests the like of which had never been tried in the SAS before. None of this really surprised me by now. I was thinking of the other poor bastards who were being put through this whole sick, bloody thing. And all so that when we were being kneecapped, we would not let on who we were.

And then they came to Gordon.

"Our attitude towards Trooper Reeve is rather ambivalent." This was the man in the white coat talking. "He's a bloody fine soldier, and give him a physical job to do and he'll do it. But he has always worked as a loner in the past, so we put the two of you together to see how you would react to sharing a cell, and, more especially, to see how Reeve would cope once his friend had been taken away from him."

Did they know of that kiss then, or did they not?

"I'm afraid," went on the doctor, "that the result may be negative. He's come to depend upon you, John, hasn't he? We are, of course, aware that you have not been dependent upon him."

"What about the screams from the other cells?"

"Tape-recordings."

I nodded, tired suddenly, uninterested.

"The whole thing was another bloody test then?"

"Of course it was." They had a little smile between them. "But that needn't bother you now. What matters is that you've passed."

It did worry me, though. What was it all about? I'd exchanged friendship for this informal debriefing. I'd exchanged love for these smirks. And Gordon's screams were still in my ears. Revenge, he was crying, revenge. I laid my hands on my knees, bent forward, and started to weep.

"You bastards," I said, "you bastards."

And if I'd had a Browning pistol with me at that moment, I'd have put large holes into their grinning skulls.

They had me checked again, more thoroughly this time, in a military hospital. Civil war had indeed broken out in Ulster, but I stared past it towards Gordon Reeve. What had happened to him? Was he still in that stinking cell, alone because of me? Was he falling apart? I took it all on my shoulders and wept again. They had given me a box of tissues. That seemed to be the way of things.

Then I started to weep all day, sometimes uncontrollably, taking it all on, taking everything on my conscience. I suffered from nightmares. I volunteered my resignation. I *demanded* my resignation. It was accepted, reluctantly. I was, after all, a guinea-pig. I went to a small fishing-village in Fife and walked along the pebbly beach, recovering from my nervous breakdown and putting the whole thing out of my mind, stuffing the most painful episode of my life into drawers and attics in my head, locking it all away, learning to forget.

So I forgot.

And they were good to me. They gave me some compensation money and they pulled a lot of strings when I decided that I wanted to join the police force. Oh yes, I could not complain about their attitude towards me, but I wasn't allowed to find out about my friend, and I wasn't ever to get in touch with them again. I was dead, I was strictly off their records.

I was a failure.

And I'm still a failure. Broken marriage. My daughter kidnapped. But it all makes sense now. The whole thing makes sense. So at least I know that Gordon is alive, if not well, and I know that he has my little girl and that he's going to kill her.

And kill me if he can.

And to get her back, I'm going to have to kill him.

And I would do it now. God help me, I would do it now.

# PART FIVE

## *Knots & Crosses*

### XXIII

When John Rebus awoke from what had seemed a particularly deep and dream-troubled sleep, he found that he was
not in bed. He saw that Michael was standing over him, a
wary smile on his face, and that Gill was pacing back and fro,
sniffing back tears.

"What happened?" said Rebus.

"Nothing," said Michael.

Then Rebus recalled that Michael had hypnotised him.

"Nothing?" cried Gill. "You call that nothing?"

"John," said Michael, "I didn't realise that you felt that way
about the old man and me. I'm sorry we made you feel bad."
Michael rested his hand on his brother's shoulder, *the brother
he had never known.*

Gordon, Gordon Reeve. What happened to you? You're all
torn and dirty, whirling around me like grit on a windswept
street. Like a brother. You've got my daughter. Where are
you?

"Oh, Jesus." Rebus let his head fall, screwing his eyes shut.
Gill's hand stroked his hair.

It was growing light outside. The birds were back into their
untiring routine. Rebus was glad that they were calling him
back into the real world. They reminded him that there
might be someone out there who was feeling happy. Perhaps
lovers awakening in each other's arms, or a man who was

realising that today was a holiday, or an elderly woman thanking God that she was alive to see the first hints of reawakening life.

"A real dark night of the soul," he said, beginning to shake. "It's cold in here. The pilot-light must have blown out."

Gill blew her nose and folded her arms.

"No, it's warm enough in here, John. Listen," she spoke slowly, deferentially, "we need a physical description of this man. I know that it will have to be a fifteen-year-old description, but it'll be a start. Then we need to check up on what happened to him after you des . . . after you left him."

"That will be classified, if it exists at all."

"And we need to tell the Chief about all of this." Gill went on as if Rebus had said nothing. Her eyes were fixed in front of her. "We need to find that creep."

The room seemed very quiet to Rebus, as though a death had occurred, when really it had been a birth of sorts, the birth of his memory. Of Gordon. Of walking out of that cold, merciless cell. Of turning his back . . .

"Can you be sure that this Reeve character is your man?" Michael was pouring more whisky. Rebus shook his head at the proffered glass.

"Not for me, thanks. My head feels all fuzzy. Oh yes, I think we can be pretty certain who's behind it. The messages, the knots and the crosses. It all makes sense now. It's been making sense all along. Reeve must think I'm really thick. He's been sending me clear messages for weeks, and I've failed to realise . . . I've let those girls die . . . All because I couldn't face the facts . . . the facts . . ."

Gill bent down behind him and put her hands on his shoulders. John Rebus shot out of his chair and turned to her. *Reeve.* No, Gill, Gill. He shook his head in mute apology. Then burst into tears.

Gill looked towards Michael, but Michael had lowered his eyes. She hugged Rebus hard, not allowing him to break away from her again, all the time whispering that it was she, Gill, beside him, and not any ghost from the past. Michael was wondering what he had got himself into. He had never seen John cry before. Again, the guilt flooded him. He would stop it all. He didn't need it any more. He would lie low and just let his dealer get tired of looking for him, let his clients find new people. He would do it, not for John's sake but for his own.

We treated him like shit, he thought to himself, it's true. The old man and me treated him as though he were an intruder.

Later, over coffee, Rebus seemed calm, though Gill's eyes were still on him, wondering, fearing.

"We can be sure that this Reeve is off his chump," she said.

"Perhaps," said Rebus. "One thing *is* for sure, he'll be armed. He'll be ready for anything. The man was a Seaforths regular and a member of the SAS. He'll be hard as nails."

"You were, too, John."

"That's why I'm the man to track him down. The Chief must be made to understand that, Gill. I'm back on the case."

Gill pursed her lips.

"I'm not sure he'll go for that," she said.

"Well, sod him then. I'll find the bastard anyway."

"You do that, John," said Michael. "You do that. Don't care what any of them say."

"Mickey," said Rebus, "you are absolutely the best brother I could have had. Now, is there any food on the go? I'm starved."

"And I'm wicked," said Michael, feeling pleased with himself. "Do you mind if I lie down for an hour or two here before I drive back?"

"Not at all, go through to my room, Mickey."

"Goodnight, Michael," said Gill.

He was smiling as he left them.

Knots and crosses. Noughts and crosses. It was so blatent, really. Reeve must have taken him for a fool, and in a way he had been right. Those endless games they had played, all those tricks and manoeuvres, and their talk about Christianity, those reef knots and Gordian knots. And The Cross. God, how stupid he had been, allowing his memory into tricking him that the past was a cracked and useless vessel, emptying its spirit. How stupid.

"John, you're spilling your coffee."

Gill was bringing in a plateful of cheese on toast from the kitchen. Rebus roused himself awake.

"Eat this. I've been on to HQ. We've to be there in two hours' time. They've already started running a check on Reeve's name. We should find him."

"I hope so, Gill. Oh God, I hope so."

They hugged. She suggested that they lie on the couch. They did so, tight in a warming embrace. Rebus couldn't help wondering whether his dark night had been an exorcism of sorts, whether the past would still haunt him sexually. He hoped not. Certainly, it was neither the time nor the place to try it out.

*Gordon my friend, what did I do to you?*

## XXIV

Stevens was a patient man. The two policemen had been firm with him. No one could see Detective Sergeant Rebus for the moment. Stevens had returned to the newspaper office, worked on a report for the paper's three-a.m. print-run, and then had driven back to Rebus's flat. There were still lights on up there, but also there were two new gorillas by the door of the tenement. Stevens parked across the street and lit another cigarette. It was tying together nicely. The two threads were becoming one. The murders and the drug-pushing were involved in some way, and Rebus was the key by the look of things. What were his brother and he talking about at this hour? A contingency plan perhaps. God, he would have given anything to be a fly on the living-room wall just now. Anything. He knew reporters in Fleet Street who went in for sophisticated surveillance techniques—bugs, high-powered microphones, telephone-taps—and he wondered if it might not be worthwhile to invest in some of that equipment himself.

He formulated new theories in his head, theories with hundreds of permutations. If Edinburgh's drug-racketeers had gone into the abduction-and-murder business to put the frights on some poor bastards, then things were taking a very grim turn indeed, and he, Jim Stevens, would have to be even more careful in future. Yet Big Podeen had known nothing. Say, then, that a new gang had broken into the game, bringing with it new rules. That would make for a gang-war, Glasgow-style. But things, surely, were not done that way today. Maybe.

In this way, Stevens kept himself awake and alert, scribbling his thoughts into a notebook. His radio was on, and he listened to the half-hourly news reports. A policeman's daughter was the new victim of Edinburgh's child-murderer. In the most recent abduction, a man was killed, strangled in the house of the child's mother. And so on. Stevens went on formulating, went on speculating.

It had not yet been revealed that *all* the murders were linked to Rebus. The police were not about to make that public, not even to Jim Stevens.

At seven-thirty, Stevens managed to bribe a passing newspaper-boy into bringing him rolls and milk from a nearby shop. He washed the dry, powdery rolls down with the icy milk. The heating was on in his car, but he felt chilled to the marrow. He needed a shower, a shave, a shit, and some sleep. Not necessarily in that order. But he was too close to let this go now. He had the tenacity—some would call it madness, fanaticism—of every good reporter. He had watched other hacks arriving in the night and being sent away again. One or two had seen him sitting in his car and had come across for a chat and to sniff out any leads. He had hidden away his notebook then, feigning disinterest, telling them that he would be going home shortly. Lies, damned lies.

That was part of the business.

And now, finally, they were emerging from the building. A few cameras and microphones were there, of course, but nothing too tasteless, no pushing and shoving and harassing. For one thing, this was a grieving father; for another, he was a policeman. Nobody was about to harass him.

Stevens watched as Gill and Rebus were allowed to disappear into the back of an idling Rover police-car. He studied their faces. Rebus looked washed-out. That was only to be expected. But, behind that, lay a grimness of look, something about the way his mouth made a straight line. That bothered Stevens a little. It was as if the man were about to enter a war. Bloody hell. And then there was Gill Templer. She looked rough, rougher even than Rebus. Her eyes were red, but here too there was something a little out of the ordinary. Something was not quite as it should be. Any respecting reporter could see that, if he knew what he was looking for. Stevens gnawed at himself. He needed to know more. It was like a drug, this story. He needed bigger and bigger injections of it. He was a bit startled, too, to find himself admitting that the reason he needed these injections was not for the sake of his job, but for his own curiosity. Rebus intrigued him. Gill Templer, of course, interested him.

And Michael Rebus . . .

Michael Rebus had not appeared from the flat. The circus was leaving now, the Rover turning right out of the quiet Marchmont Street, but the gorillas remained. New gorillas. Stevens lit a cigarette. It might be worth a try at that. He walked back to his car and locked it. Then, taking a walk round the block, formed another plan.

"Excuse me, sir. Do you live here?"

"Of course I live here! What's all this about, eh? I need to get to my bed."

"Had a heavy night, sir?"

The bleary-eyed man shook three brown paper-bags at the policeman. The bags each contained six rolls.

"I'm a baker. Shift-work. Now if you'll . . ."

"And your name, sir?"

Making to pass the man, Stevens had just had time enough to make out a few of the names on the door-buzzer.

"Laidlaw," he said. "Jim Laidlaw."

The policeman checked this against a list of names in his hand.

"All right, sir. Sorry to have bothered you."

"What's all this about?"

"You'll find out soon enough, sir. Good night now."

There was one more obstacle, and Stevens knew that for all his cunning, if the door was locked then the door was locked, and his game was up. He made a plausible push at the heavy door and felt it give. They had not locked it. His patron saint was smiling on him today.

In the tenement hallway, he ditched the rolls and thought of another ploy. He climbed the two flights of stairs to Rebus's door. The tenement seemed to smell exclusively of cats'-piss. At Rebus's door he paused, catching his breath. Partly, he was out of condition, but partly, also, he was excited. He had not felt anything like this on a story for years. It felt good. He decided that he could get away with anything on a day like this. He pushed the doorbell relentlessly.

The door was opened at last by a yawning, puffy-faced Michael Rebus. So at last they were face to face. Stevens flashed a card at Michael. The card identified James Stevens as a member of an Edinburgh snooker club.

"Detective Inspector Stevens, sir. Sorry to get you out of bed." He put the card away. "Your brother told us that you'd probably still be asleep, but I thought I'd come up anyway. May I come in? Just a few questions, sir. Won't keep you too long."

The two policemen, their feet numb despite thermal socks and the fact that it was the beginning of summer, shuffled one foot and then the other, hoping for a reprieve. The talk was all of the abduction and the fact that a Chief Inspector's son had been murdered. The main door opened behind them.

"You lot still here? The wife told me there was bobbies at the door, but I didnae believe her. Yon wis last night, though. What's the matter?"

This was an old man, still in his slippers but with a thick, winter overcoat on. He was half-shaven only, and his bottom false-teeth had been lost or forgotten about. He was attaching a cap to his bald head as he sidled out of the door.

"Nothing for you to worry about, sir. You'll be told soon enough, I'm sure."

"Oh aye, well then. I'm just away to fetch the paper and the milk. We usually have toast for breakfast, but some bugger's gone and left about twa dozen new rolls in the lobby. Well, if they're no' wanted, they're aye welcome in my house."

He chuckled, showing the raw red of his bottom gum.

"Can I get you twa anything at the shop?"

But the two policemen were staring at one another, alarmed, speechless.

"Get up there," one said, finally, to the other. Then: "And your name, sir?"

"Jock Laidlaw," he said, "at your service."

Stevens was drinking, thankfully, the black coffee. The first hot thing he'd had in ages. He was seated in the living-room, his eyes everywhere.

"I'm glad you woke me," Michael Rebus was saying. "I've got to get back home."

I'll bet you have, thought Stevens. I'll bet you have. Rebus looked altogether more relaxed than he had foreseen. Relaxed, rested, easy with his conscience. Curiouser and curiouser.

"Just a few questions, Mister Rebus, as I said."

Michael Rebus sat down, crossing his legs, sipping his own coffee.

"Yes?"

Stevens produced his notebook.

"Your brother has had a very great shock."

"Yes."

"But he'll be all right you think?"

"Yes."

Stevens pretended to write in his book.

"Did he have a good night, by the way? Did he sleep all right?"

"Well, none of us got much sleep. I'm not sure John slept at all." Michael's eyebrows were gathering. "Look, what is all this?"

"Just routine, Mister Rebus. You understand. We need all the details from everyone involved if we're going to crack this case."

"But it's cracked, isn't it?"

Stevens's heart jumped.

"Is it?" he heard himself say.

"Well, don't you know?"

"Yes, of course, but we have to get *all* the details—"

"From everyone concerned. Yes, so you said. Look, can I see your identification again? Just to be on the safe side."

There was the sound of a key prodding at the front door.

Christ, thought Stevens, they're back already.

"Listen," he said through his teeth, "we know all about your little drugs-racket. Now tell us who's behind it or else we'll put you behind bars for a hundred years, sonny!"

Michael's face went light-blue, then grey. His mouth seemed ready to drop open with a word, the one word Stevens needed.

But then one of the gorillas was in the room, propelling Stevens out of his chair.

"I've not finished my coffee yet!" he protested.

"You're lucky I don't break your flaming neck, pal," replied the policeman.

Michael Rebus stood up, too, but he was saying nothing.

"A name!" cried Stevens. "Just give me the name! This'll be spread right across the front pages, my friend, if you don't co-operate! Give me the name!"

He kept up his cries all the way down the stairwell. Right down to the last step.

"All right, I'm going," he said eventually, breaking free of the heavy grip on his arm. "I'm going. You were a bit slack there, boys, weren't you? I'll keep it quiet this time, but next time you better be ready. Okay?"

"Get out of here," said one gorilla.

Stevens did. He slid into his car, feeling more frustrated and more curious than ever. God, he'd been close. But what did the hypnotist mean by that? The case was cracked. Was it? If so, he wanted to be there with the first details. He was not used to being so far behind in the game. Usually, games were played by his rules. No, he was not used to this, and he did not like it at all.

He loved it.

But, if the case was cracked, then time was tight. And if you could not get what you wanted from one brother, then go to the other. He thought he knew where John Rebus would be. His intuition ran high today. He felt inspired.

## XXV

"Well, John, this all seems quite fantastical, but I'm sure it's a possibility. Certainly, it's the best lead we've got, though I find it hard to conceive of a man with so much hate that he would murder four innocent girls just to give you the clues as to his ultimate victim."

Chief Superintendent Wallace looked from Rebus to Gill Templer and back again. To Rebus's left sat Anderson. Wallace's hands lay like dead fish on his desk, a pen in front of him. The room was large and uncluttered, a self-assured oasis. Here, problems were always solved, decisions were made—always correctly.

"The problem now is finding him. If we make this thing public, then that might scare him off, endangering your daughter's life in the process. On the other hand, a public appeal would be by far the quickest way of finding him."

"You can't possibly . . . !" It was Gill Templer who, in that quiet room, was on the verge of exploding, but Wallace silenced her with a wave of his hand.

"I am merely thinking aloud at this stage, Inspector Templer, merely casting stones into a pond."

Anderson sat like a corpse, his eyes to the floor. He was on leave now officially and in mourning, but he had insisted on keeping in touch with the case and Superintendent Wallace had acquiesced.

"Of course, John," Wallace was saying, "it's impossible for you to remain on the case."

Rebus rose to his feet.

"Sit down, John, please." The Super's eyes were hard and honest, the eyes of a real copper, one of the old school. Rebus sat down again. "Now I know how you must feel, believe it or believe it not. But there's too much at stake here. Too much for all of us. You're far too involved to be of any objective use, and the public would cry out about vigilante tactics. You must see that."

"All I see is that without me Reeve will stop at nothing. It's me he wants."

"Exactly. And wouldn't we be stupid to hand you over to him on a plate? We'll do everything we can, as much as you could do. Leave it to us."

"The Army won't tell you anything, you know."

"They'll have to." Wallace began to toy with his pen, as though it were there for that very purpose. "Ultimately, they've got the same boss we have. They'll be made to tell."

Rebus shook his head.

"They're a law unto themselves. The SAS is hardly even a part of the Army. If they don't want to tell you, then believe me, they won't tell you a bloody thing." Rebus's hand came down onto the desk. "Not a bloody thing."

"John." Gill's hand squeezed his shoulder, asking him to be calm. She herself looked like a fury, but she knew when to keep quiet and let looks alone transmit her anger and her displeasure. For Rebus, however, it was actions that counted. He'd been sitting outside reality for way too long.

He rose from his small chair like a pure force, no longer human, and left the room in silence. The Superintendent looked at Gill.

"He's off the case, Gill. He must be made to realise that. I believe that you," he paused while opening and shutting a drawer, "that you and he have an understanding. That, at least, is how we used to phrase it in my day. Perhaps you should make him aware of his position. We'll get this man, but not with Rebus hanging around intent on revenge." Wallace looked towards Anderson, who stared drily at him. "We don't want vigilante tactics," he went on. "Not in Edinburgh. What would the tourists say?" Then his face broke into a cold smile. He looked from Anderson to Gill, then rose from his chair. "This is all becoming extremely . . ."

"Internecine?" suggested Gill.

"I was going to say incestuous. What with Chief Inspector Anderson here, his son and Rebus's wife, yourself and Rebus, Rebus and this man Reeve, Reeve and Rebus's daughter. I hope the press don't get wind of this. You'll be responsible for seeing that they don't, and for pushing any that do. Am I making myself clear?"

Gill Templer nodded, stifling a sudden yawn.

"Good." The Super nodded across to Anderson. "Now see that Chief Inspector Anderson gets home safely, will you?"

William Anderson, seated in the back of the car, went through his mental list of informants and friends. He knew a couple of people who might know about the Special Air Squadron. Certainly, something like the Rebus–Reeve case could not have been hushed up totally, though it might well have been struck from the records. The soldiers would have known about it though. Grapevines existed everywhere, and especially where you would least expect them. He might need to twist a few arms and lay out a few tenners, but he would find the bastard if it was his last action on God's earth.

Or he would be there when Rebus did.

Rebus had left the HQ by a back entrance, as Stevens had hoped. He followed Rebus as the policeman, looking the worse for wear, stalked away. What was it all about? No matter. As long as he stuck to Rebus, he could be sure of getting his story, and what a story it promised to be. Stevens kept checking behind him, but there seemed to be no tail on Rebus. No police tail, that was. It seemed strange to him that they would allow Rebus to go off on his own when there was no telling what a man would do whose daughter had been abducted. Stevens was hoping for the ultimate plot: he was hoping that Rebus would lead him straight to the big boys behind this new drugs ring. If not one brother, then the other.

Like a brother to me, and I to him. What happened? He knew what was to blame at heart. The method, that was the cause of all of this. The caging and the breaking and then the patching up. The patching up had not been a success, had it? They were both broken men in their own ways. That knowledge wouldn't stop him from shearing Reeve's head from its shoulders, though. Nothing would stop that. But he had to find the bastard yet, and he had no idea where to start. He could feel the city closing in on him, bringing to bear all of its historical weight, smothering him. Dissent, rationalism, enlightenment: Edinburgh had specialized in all three, and now he, too, would need these charms. He needed to work on his own, quickly, yet methodically, using ingenuity and every tool at his disposal. Most of all he needed instinct.

After five minutes, he knew he was being followed, and the hair stood up at the back of his neck. It was not the usual police tail. That would not have been so easy to spot. But was it . . . Could he be so close . . . At a bus-stop, he stopped and turned suddenly, as though checking to see if a bus was coming. He saw the man dodge into a doorway. It wasn't Gordon Reeve. It was that bloody reporter.

Rebus listene 1 to his heart slow again, but the adrenalin was already pumping through him, filling him with a desire to run, to take off along this long straight road and run into the strongest head-wind imaginable. But then a bus came trundling round the corner, and he boarded that instead.

From the back window, he saw the reporter jump out of the doorway and desperately flag down a taxi-cab. Rebus had no time to be bothered with the man. He had some thinking to do, thinking about how in the world he could find Reeve. The possibility haunted him: he'll find *me*. I don't need to chase. But somehow that scared him most of all.

Gill Templer could not find Rebus. He had disappeared as though he had been a shadow merely and not a man at all. She telephone and hunted and asked and did all the things a good copper should do, but she was confronted by the fact of a man who was not only a good copper himself, but had been one of the best in the SAS to boot. He might have been hiding under her feet, under her desk, in her clothes, and she would never have found him. So he stayed hidden.

He stayed hidden, she surmised, because he was on the move, swiftly and methodically moving through the streets and bars of Edinburgh in search of his prey, knowing that when found, the prey would turn hunter once more.

But Gill went on trying, shivering now and then when she thought of her lover's grim and horrific past, and of the mentality of those who decided that such things were necessary. Poor John. What would she have done? She would have walked right out of that cell and kept on walking, just as he had done. And yet she would have felt guilty, too, just as he had felt guilt, and she would have put it all behind her, scarred invisibly.

Why did the men in her life have to be such complicated, fraught, screwed-up bastards? Did she attract the soiled goods only? It might have been humorous, but then there was Sa-

mantha to think about, and that wasn't funny at all. Where did
you start looking if you wanted to find a needle? She remembered Superintendent Wallace's words: *they've got the same
boss we have.* That was a truth well worth contemplating in all
its complexity. For if they had the same boss, then perhaps a
cover-up could be arranged at this end, now that the ancient
and terrible truth had surfaced again. If this got into the
papers, all Hell would be let loose at every level of the service.
Perhaps they would want to co-operate in hushing it up. Perhaps they would want Rebus silenced. My God, what if they
should want John Rebus silenced? That would mean silencing
Anderson, too, and herself. It would mean bribes or a total
wipe-out. She would have to be very careful indeed. One false
move now might mean her dismissal from the force, and that
would not do at all. Justice had to be seen to be done. There
could be no cover-ups. The Boss, whoever or whatever that
anonymous term was meant to imply, would not have his or
its day. There had to be truth, or the whole thing was a sham,
and so were its actors.

And what of her feelings towards John Rebus himself, spot-
lit on the reddened stage? She hardly knew what to think.
The notion still niggled at her that, no matter how absurd it
might appear, John was somehow behind this whole thing: no
Reeve, the notes sent to himself, jealousy leading him to kill
his wife's lover, his daughter now hidden somewhere—somewhere like that locked room.

It was hardly to be contemplated, which, considering the
way the whole thing had gone thus far, was why Gill contemplated it very hard indeed. And rejected it, rejected it for no
other reason than that John Rebus had once made love to her,
once bared his soul to her, once clasped her hand beneath a
hospital blanket. Would a man with something to hide have
become involved with a policewoman? No, it seemed wholly
unlikely.

So, again, it became a possibility, joining the others. Gill's
head began to pulse. Where the hell was John? And what if
Reeve found him before they found Reeve? If John Rebus was

a walking beacon to his enemy, then wasn't it crazy for him to be out there on his own, wherever he was? Of course it was stupid. It had been stupid to let him walk out of the room, out of the building, vanishing like a whisper. Shit. She picked up the telephone again and dialled his flat.


## XXVI

John Rebus was moving through the jungle of the city, that jungle the tourists never saw, being too busy snapping away at the ancient golden temples, temples long since gone but still evident as shadows. This jungle closed in on the tourists relentlessly but unseen, a natural force, the force of dissipation and destruction.

Edinburgh's an easy beat, his colleagues from the west coast would say. Try Patrick for a night and tell me that it's not. But Rebus knew different. He knew that Edinburgh was all appearances, which made the crime less easy to spot, but no less evident. Edinburgh was a schizophrenic city, the place of Jekyll & Hyde sure enough, the city of Deacon Brodie, of fur coats and no knickers (as they said in the west). But it was a small city, too, and that would be to Rebus's advantage.

He hunted in the hard-man's drinking dens, in the housing estates where heroin and unemployment were the totem kings, for he knew that somewhere in this anonymity a hard man could hide and could plan and could survive. He was trying to get inside Gordon Reeve's skin. It was a skin sloughed many times, and Rebus had to admit, finally, that he was further away from his insane, murderous blood-brother than ever before. If he had turned his back on Gordon Reeve, then Reeve was refusing to show himself anyway. Perhaps there would be another note, another teasing clue. Oh, Sammy, Sammy, Sammy. Please God let her live, let her live.

Gordon Reeve had levitated right out of Rebus's world. He was floating overhead, floating and gloating in his new-found power. It had taken him fifteen years to accomplish his trick,

but my God what a trick. Fifteen years within which time he
had probably changed his name and appearance, taken on a
menial job, researched Rebus's life. How long had this man
been watching him? Watching and hating and scheming? All
those times that he had felt his flesh creep for no reason, that
the telephone had rung without a voice behind it, that small,
easily forgotten accidents had occurred. And Reeve, grinning
above him, a little god over Rebus's destiny. Rebus, shivering,
entered a pub for the hell of it and ordered a triple whisky.

"It's quarter-gills in here, pal. Are you sure you want a
treble?"

"Sure."

What the hell. It was all one. If God swirled in his heaven,
leaning down to touch his creatures, then it was a curious
touch indeed that he gave them. Looking around, Rebus
stared into a heart of desperation. Old men sat with their half-
pint glasses, staring emptily towards the front door. Were
they wondering what was outside? Or were they just scared
that whatever was out there would one day force its way in,
pushing into their dark corners and cowered glances with the
wrath of some Old Testament monster, some behemoth,
some flood of destruction? Rebus could not see behind their
eyes, just as they could not see behind his. That ability not to
share the sufferings of others was all that kept the mass of
humanity rolling on, concentrating on the "me," shunning
the beggars and their folded arms. Rebus, behind his eyes,
was begging now, begging to that strange God of his to allow
him to find Reeve, to explain himself to the madman. God did
not answer. The TV blared out some banal quiz show.

"Fight Imperialism, fight Racism."

A young girl wearing a mock-leather coat and little round
glasses stood behind Rebus. He turned to her. She had a collecting tin in one hand and a pile of newspapers in the other.

"Fight Imperialism, fight Racism."

"So you said." Even now he could feel the alcohol working
on his jaw muscles, freeing them of stiffness. "Who are you
from?"

"Workers Revolutionary Party. The only way to smash the Imperialist system is for the workers to unite and smash Racism. Racism is the backbone of repression."

"Oh? Aren't you confusing two entirely different arguments there, love?"

She bristled, but was ready to argue. They always were.

"The two are inextricable. Capitalism was built on slave labour and is maintained by slave labour."

"You don't sound much like a slave, dear. Where did you get that accent? Cheltenham?"

"My father was a slave to capitalist ideology. He didn't know what he was doing."

"You mean you went to an expensive school?"

She was bristling now, all right. Rebus lit a cigarette. He offered her one, but she shook her head. A capitalist product, he supposed, the leaves picked by slaves in South America. She was quite pretty though. Eighteen, nineteen. Funny Victorian shoes on, tight, pointed little things. A long, straight black skirt. Black, the colour of dissent. He was all for dissent.

"You're a student, I suppose?"

"That's right," she said, shuffling uncomfortably. She knew a buyer when she saw one. This was not a buyer.

"Edinburgh University?"

"Yes."

"Studying what?"

"English and politics."

"English? Have you heard of a guy called Eiser? He teaches there."

She nodded.

"What was your party again?"

"Workers Revolutionary."

"But you're a student, eh? Not a worker, not one of the proletariat, either, by the sound of you." Her face was red, her eyes burning fire. Come the revolution, Rebus would be first against the wall. But he had not yet played his trump card. "So really, you're contravening the Trades Description Act, aren't you? And what about that tin? Do you have a licence from the proper authority to collect money in that tin?"

The tin was old, its old job-description torn from it. It was a plain, red cylinder, the kind used on poppy-day. But this was no poppy-day.

"Are you a cop?"

"Got it in one, love. *Have* you got a licence? I may have to pull you in otherwise."

"Sodding pig!"

Feeling this a fitting exit line, she turned from Rebus and walked to the door. Rebus, chuckling, finished his whisky. Poor girl. She would change. The idealism would vanish once she saw how hypocritical the whole game was, and what luxuries lay outside university. When she left, she'd want it all: the executive job in London, the flat, car, salary, wine-bar. She would chuck it all in for a slice of pie. But she wouldn't understand that just now. Now was for the reaction against upbringing. That was what university was about. They all thought they could change the world once they got away from their parents. Rebus had thought that, too. He had thought to return home from the Army with a row of medals and a list of commendations, just to show them. It had not been that way, though. Chastened, he was about to go when a voice called to him from three or four bar-stools away.

"It disnae cure anything, dis it, son?"

An aged crone offered him these few pearls of wisdom from her cavernous mouth. Rebus watched her tongue slopping around in that black cavern.

"Aye," he said, paying the barman, who thanked him with green teeth. Reeve could hear the television, the jingle of the cash-register, the shouted conversations of the old men, but behind it all, behind the cacophony, lay another sound, low and pure but more real to him than any of the others.

It was the sound of Gordon Reeve screaming.

*Let me out Let me out*

But Rebus did not go dizzy this time, nor did he panic and run for it. He stood up to the sound and allowed it to make its point, let it wash over him until it had had its say. He would never run away from that memory again.

"Drink never cured anything, son," continued his personal witch. "Look at me. I wis as guid as anybody once upon a time, but when my husband died I just went tae pieces. D'ye ken whit I mean, son? The drink wis a great comfort tae me then, or so I thocht. But it tricks ye. It plays games wi ye. Ye jist sit aw day daein' nothing but drinking. And life passes ye by."

She was right. How could he take the time to sit here guzzling whisky and sentiment when his daughter's life was balanced so finely? He must be mad; he was losing reality again. He had to hang onto that at the very least. He could pray again, but that only seemed to take him further away from the brute facts, and it was facts that he was chasing now, not dreams. He was chasing the fact that a lunatic from his cupboard of bad dreams had sneaked into this world and carried off his daughter. Did it resemble a fairy tale? All the better: there was bound to be a happy ending.

"You're right, love," he said. Then, ready to leave, he pointed to her empty glass. "Want another of those?"

She stared at him through rheumy eyes, then wagged her chin in a parody of compliance.

"Another of what the lady's drinking," Rebus said to the green-toothed barman. He handed over some coins. "And give her the change." Then he left the bar.

"I need to talk. I think you do, too."

Stevens was lighting a cigarette, rather melodramatically to Rebus's mind, directly outside the bar. Beneath the glare of the street-lighting, his skin seemed almost yellow, seemed hardly thick enough to cover his skull.

"Well, can we talk?" The reporter put his lighter back in his pocket. His fair hair looked greasy. He had not shaved for a day or so. He looked hungry and cold.

But inside, he felt electric.

"You've led me a merry dance, Mister Rebus. Can I call you John?"

"Look, Stevens, you know the score here. I've got enough on my plate without all this."

Rebus made to move past the reporter, but Stevens caught his arm.

"No," he said, "I *don't* know the score, not the final score. I seem to have been ejected from the park at half-time."

"What do you mean?"

"You know exactly who's behind all this, don't you? Of course you do, and so do your superiors. Or do they? Have you told them the whole truth and nothing but the truth, John? Have you told them about Michael?"

"What about him?"

"Oh, come on." Stevens started to shuffle his feet, looking around him at the high blocks of flats, the late-afternoon sky behind them. He chuckled, shivering. Rebus recalled seeing him make that curious shivery motion at the party. "Where can we talk?" said the reporter now. "What about in the pub? Or is there someone in there you'd rather I didn't see?"

"Stevens, you're off your head. I'm serious. Go home, get some sleep, eat, have a bath, just get to hell away from me. Okay?"

"Or you'll do what, exactly? Get your brother's heavy friend to rough me up a little? Listen, Rebus, the game's over. I *know*. But I don't know all of it. You'd be wise to have me as a friend rather than an enemy. Don't take me for a monkey. I credit you with more sense than to do that. Don't let me down."

*Don't let me down*

"After all, they've got your daughter. You need my help. I've got friends everywhere. We've got to fight this together."

Rebus, confused, shook his head.

"I don't have a bloody clue what you're talking about, Stevens. Go home, will you?"

Jim Stevens sighed, shaking his own head ruefully. He threw his cigarette onto the pavement and stubbed it out heavily, sending little flares of burning tobacco across the concrete.

"Well, I'm sorry, John. I really am. Michael's going to be put behind bars for a very long time on the evidence I have against him."

"Evidence? Of what?"

"His drug-pushing, of course."

Stevens didn't see the blow coming. It wouldn't have helped it he had. It was a vicious, curving swipe, sweeping up from Rebus's side and catching him very low in the stomach. The reporter coughed out a little puff of wind, then fell to his knees.

"Liar! Bloody liar!"

Stevens coughed and coughed. It was as if he had run a marathon. He gulped in air, staying on his knees, his arms folded in front of his belly.

"If you say so, John, but it's true, anyway." He looked up at Rebus. "You mean you honestly don't know anything about it? Nothing it all?"

"You better have some good proof, Stevens, or I'm going to see you swing."

Stevens hadn't expected this, he hadn't expected this at all.

"Well," he said, "this puts a different complexion on everything. Christ, I need a drink. Will you join me? I think we should talk a little now, don't you? I won't keep you long, but I think you should know."

And, of course, thinking back, Rebus realised that he had known, but not consciously. That day, the day of the old man's death, of visiting the rain-soaked graveyard, of visiting Mickey, he had smelled that toffee-apple smell in the living-room. He knew now what it had been. He had thought of it then, but had been distracted. Jesus Christ. Rebus felt his whole world sinking into the morass of a personal madness. He hoped the breakdown was not far off; he couldn't keep going on like this for much longer.

Toffee-apples, fairy-tales, Sammy, Sammy, Sammy. Sometimes it was hard to hold onto reality when that reality was overpowering. The shield came to protect you. The shield of the breakdown, of forgetting. Laughter and forgetting.

"This round's on me," said Rebus, feeling calm again.

Gill Templer knew what she had always known: there was method in the killer's choice of girls, so he must have had access to their names prior to the abductions. That meant that the four girls had to have something in common, some way that Reeve could have picked them all out. But what? They had checked up on everything. Certain hobbies the girls did have in common: netball, pop music, books.

Netball. Pop music. Books.

Netball. Pop music. Books.

That meant checking through netball-coaches (all women, so scratch that), record-shop workers and DJs, and bookshop-workers and librarians. Libraries.

Libraries.

Rebus had told stories to Reeve. Samantha used the city's main lending library. So, occasionally, had the other girls. One of the girls had been seen heading up The Mound towards the library on the day she disappeared.

But Jack Morton had checked the library already. One of the men there had owned a blue Ford Escort. The suspect had been passed over. But had that initial interview been enough? She had to speak to Morton. Then she would conduct a second interview herself. She was about to look for Morton when her telephone rang.

"Inspector Templer," she said to the beige mouthpiece.

"The kid dies tonight," hissed a voice on the other end.

She sat bolt upright in her chair, almost causing it to topple.

"Listen," she said, "if you're a crank . . ."

"Shut up, bitch. I'm no crank and you know it. I'm the real thing. Listen." There was a muffled cry from somewhere, the sob of a young girl. Then the hiss returned. "Tell Rebus tough luck. He can't say I never gave him a chance."

"Listen, Reeve, I . . ."

She had not meant to say that, had not meant to let him

know. But she had panicked on hearing Samantha's cry. Now she heard another cry, the banshee cry of the madman who has been discovered. It sent the hairs on her neck climbing up each other. It froze the air around her. It was the cry of Death itself in one of its many guises. It was a lost soul's final triumphant scream.

"You know," he gasped, his voice a mixture of joy and terror, "you know, you know, you know. Aren't you clever? And you've got a very sexy voice, too. Maybe I'll come for you sometime. Was Rebus a good lay? Was he? Tell him that I've got his baby, and she dies tonight. Got that? Tonight."

"Listen, I . . ."

"No, no, no. No more from me, Miss Templer. You've had nearly long enough to trace this. Bye."

Click. Brrrr.

Time to trace it. She had been stupid. She should have thought of that first; indeed, she had not thought of it at all. Perhaps Superintendent Wallace had been right. Perhaps it was not only John who was too emotionally involved in the whole affair. She felt tired and old and spent. She felt as if all the case-work was suddenly an impossible burden, all the criminals invincible. Her eyes were irritating her. She thought of putting on her glasses, her personal shield from the world.

She had to find Rebus. Or should she seek out Jack Morton first? John would have to be told of this. They had a little time, but not much. The first guess had to be the right one. Who first? Rebus or Morton? She made the decision: John Rebus.

Unnerved by Stevens's revelations, Rebus made his way back to his flat. He needed to find out about some things. Mickey could wait. He had drawn too many bad cards in the course of his afternoon's foot-slogging. He had to get in touch with his old employers, the Army. He had to make them see that a life was at stake, they who prized life so strangely. A lot of phone-calls might be necessary. So be it.

But the first call he made was to the hospital. Rhona was

fine. That was a relief. Still, however, she had not been told of
Sammy's abduction. Rebus swallowed hard. Had she been
told of her lover's death? She had not. Of course not. He
arranged for some flowers to be sent to her. He was about to
pluck up the courage to telephone the first of a long list of
numbers when his own telephone rang. He let it ring for a
while, but the caller was not about to let him go.

"Hello?"

"John! Thank God. I've been looking for you everywhere."
It was Gill, sounding excited and nervous and yet trying to
sound sympathetic, too. Her voice modulated wildly, and Rebus felt his heart—what was left of it for public consumption
—go out to her.

"What is it, Gill? Has anything happened?"

"I've had a call from Reeve."

Rebus's heart pounded against the walls of its cell. "Tell
me," he said.

"Well, he just phoned up and said that he's got Samantha."

"And?"

Gill swallowed hard. "And that he's going to kill her tonight." There was a pause at Rebus's end, strange distant
sounds of movement. "John? Hello, John?"

Rebus stopped punching the telephone-stool. "Yes, I'm
here. Jesus Christ. Did he say anything else?"

"John, you really shouldn't be on your own, you know. I
could—"

"Did he say anything else?" He was shouting now, his
breath short like a runner's.

"Well, I . . ."

"Yes?"

"I let slip that we know who he is."

Rebus sucked in his breath, examining his knuckles, noting
that he had worn one of them open. He sucked blood, staring
from his window. "What was his reaction to that?" he said at
last.

"He went wild."

"I'll bet he did. Jesus, I hope he doesn't take it out on . . ."

Oh, Jesus. Why do you suppose he phoned you specifically?" He had stopped licking his wound, and now turned his attention on his dark fingernails, tearing at them with his teeth, spitting them out across the room.

"Well, I am Liaison Officer on the case. He may have seen me on the television or read my name in the newspapers."

"Or maybe he's seen us together. He may have been following me during this whole thing." He looked from his window as a shabbily-dressed man shuffled his way up the street, stopping to pick up a cigarette-end. Christ, he needed a cigarette. He looked around for an ashtray, source of a few re-usable butts.

"I never thought of that."

"How the hell could you? We didn't know that any of this was to do with me until . . . it was yesterday, wasn't it? It seems like days ago. But remember, Gill, his notes were delivered by hand in the beginning." He lit the remnants of a cigarette, sucking in the stinging smoke. "He's been so close to me, and I didn't feel a thing, not a tingle. So much for a policeman's sixth sense."

"Speaking of sixth senses, John, I've had a hunch." Gill was relieved to hear how his voice had become calmer. She felt a little calmer, too, as though they were helping each other to hang on to a crowded lifeboat in a storm-torn sea.

"What's that?" Rebus slumped himself into his chair, looking around his barren room, dusty and chaotic. He saw the glass used by Michael, a plate of toast crumbs, two empty cigarette packets, and two coffee cups. He would sell this place soon, no matter how low the price. He would move well away from here. He would.

"Libraries," Gill was saying, staring at her own office, the files and mounds of paperwork, the clutter of months and years, the electric buzz in the air. "The one thing that all the girls, Samantha included, have in common is that they used, if irregularly, the same library, the Central Library. Reeve might have worked there once and been able to find the names he needed to fit his puzzle."

"That's certainly a thought," said Rebus, suddenly interested. It was too much of a coincidence, surely—or was it? How better to find out about John Rebus than to get a quiet job for a few months or a few years? How better to trap young girls than by posing as a librarian? Reeve had gone undercover all right, so well camouflaged as to be invisible.

"It just happens," Gill continued, "that your friend Jack Morton has been to the Central Library already. He checked up on a suspect there who owned a blue Escort. He gave the man a clean bill of health."

"Yes, and they gave the Yorkshire Ripper a clean bill of health on more than one occasion, didn't they? It's worth rechecking. What was the suspect's name?"

"I've no idea. I've been trying to find Jack Morton, but he's off somewhere. John, I've been worried about you. Where have you been? I've been trying to find you."

"I call that a waste of police time and effort, Inspector Templer. Get your nose back to the *real* grindstone. Find Jack. Find that name."

"Yes, sir."

"I'll be here for a while if you need me. I've got a few phone calls of my own to make."

"I hear that Rhona is stable . . ." But Rebus had already put down his receiver. Gill sighed, rubbing at her face, desperate for some rest. She decided to arrange for someone to be sent over to John Rebus's flat. He could not be left to fester and, perhaps, explode. Then she had to find that name. She had to find Jack Morton.

Rebus made himself some coffee, thought about going out for milk, but decided in the end to have the coffee bitter and black, the taste and the colour of his thoughts. He thought over Gill's idea. Reeve as a librarian? It seemed improbable, unthinkable. Rationality could be a powerful enemy when you were faced with the irrational. Fight fire with fire. Accept that Gordon Reeve might have secured a job in the library; something innocuous yet essential to his plan. And suddenly, for John Rebus as for Gill, it all seemed to fit. "For those who read between the time." For those who are involved with books between one time (The Cross) and another (the present). My God, was nothing arbitrary in this life? No, nothing at all. Behind the seemingly irrational lay the clear golden path of the design. Behind this world there was another. Reeve was in the library: Rebus felt sure of that. It was five o'clock. He could reach the library just as it was closing. But would Gordon Reeve still be there, or would he have moved on now that he had his final victim?

But Rebus knew that Sammy was not Reeve's final victim. She was not a "victim" at all. She was merely another device. There could be only one victim: Rebus himself. And for that reason Reeve would still be nearby, still within Rebus's reach. For Reeve wanted to be found, but slowly, a sort of cat-and-mouse game in reverse. Rebus thought back to the game of cat-and-mouse as played in his schooldays. Sometimes the boy being chased by a girl, or the girl being chased by a boy, would want to be caught, because he or she felt something for the chaser. And so the whole thing became something other than it seemed. That was Reeve's game. Cat and mouse, and he the mouse with the sting in his tail, the bite in his teeth, and Rebus as soft as milk, as pliant as fur and contentment. There had been no contentment for Gordon Reeve, not for many years, not since he had been betrayed by one whom he had come to call brother.

*Just a kiss*

The mouse caught.

*The brother I never had*

Poor Gordon Reeve, balancing on that slender pipe, the piss trickling down his legs, and everybody laughing at him.

And poor John Rebus, shunned by his father and his brother, a brother who had turned to crime now and who must be punished eventually.

And poor Sammy. She was the one he should be thinking of. Think only of her, John, and everything will turn out all right.

But if this was a serious game, a game of life and death, then

he had to remember that it was still a game. Rebus knew now
that he had Reeve. But having caught him, what would happen? The roles would switch in some way. He did not yet
know all the rules. There was one way and only the one way to
learn them. He left the coffee to go cold on his coffee-table,
beside all the other waste. There was bitterness enough in his
mouth as it was.

And out there, out in the iron-grey drizzle, there was a
game to be finished.

## XXVII

From his flat in Marchmont to the library could be a delightful
walk, showing the strengths of Edinburgh as a city. He passed
through a verdant open area called The Meadows, and on the
skyline before him stood the great grey Castle, a flag blowing
in the fine rain over its ramparts. He passed the Royal Infir-
mary, home of discoveries and famous names, part of the
University, Greyfriar's Kirkyard and the tiny statue of
Greyfriar's Bobby. How many years had that little dog lain
beside its master's grave? How many years had Gordon Reeve
gone to sleep at night with burning thoughts of John Rebus on
his mind? He shuddered. Sammy, Sammy, Sammy. He hoped
that he would get to know his daughter better. He hoped that
he would be able to tell her that she was beautiful, and that
she would find great love in her life. Dear God, he hoped she
was alive.

Walking along George IV Bridge, which took tourists and
others over the city's Grassmarket, safely away from that area's tramps and derelicts, latter-day paupers with nowhere to
turn, John Rebus's mind churned a few facts. For one, Reeve
would be armed. For another, he might be in disguise. He
remembered Sammy talking about the down-and-outs who
sat around all day in the library. He could be one of them. He
wondered what he would do if and when he met Reeve face
to face. What would he say? Questions and theories began to

disturb him, frightened him almost as much as did the recognition that Sammy's fate at the hands of Reeve would be painful and protracted. But she was more important to him than memory: she was the future. And so he stalked towards the Gothic façade of the library with determination, not fear, on his face.

A news-vendor outside, his coat wrapped around him like damp tissue-paper, cried out the latest news, not of The Strangler today but of some disaster at sea. News did not last for long. Rebus swerved past the man, eyeing his face carefully. He noticed that his own shoes were letting in water as usual, then he entered the oak swing-doors.

At the main desk a security man flicked through a newspaper. He did not resemble Gordon Reeve, not in any way at all. Rebus breathed deeply, trying to stop himself from shaking.

"We're closing, sir," said the guard from behind his newspaper.

"Yes, I'm sure you are." The guard did not appear to like the sound of Rebus's voice; it was a hard, icy voice, used like a weapon. "My name's Rebus. Detective Sergeant Rebus. I'm looking for a man called Reeve who works here. Is he around?"

Rebus hoped that he sounded calm. He did not feel calm. The guard left his newspaper on the chair and came up to face him. He studied Rebus, as though wary of him. Good: Rebus wanted it that way.

"Can I see your identification?"

Clumsily, his fingers not ready to be delicate, Rebus fished out his ID card. The guard looked at it for some time, glancing up at him.

"Reeve, did you say?" He handed Rebus's card back and brought out a list of names attached to a yellow plastic clipboard. "Reeve, Reeve, Reeve. No, there's nobody called Reeve works here."

"Are you sure? He may not be a librarian. He could be a cleaner or something, anything."

"No, everybody's on my list, from the Director down to the porter. Look, that's my name there. Simpson. Everybody's on this list. He'd be on this list if he worked here. You must have made a mistake."

Staff were beginning to leave the building, calling out their "goodnight's and their "see you's. He might lose Reeve if he didn't hurry. Always supposing that Reeve still worked here. It was such a slender straw, such a tenuous hope, that Rebus began to panic again.

"Can I see that list?" He put out his hand, making his eyes burn with authority. The guard hesitated, then handed over the clipboard. Rebus searched it furiously, looking for anagrams, clues, anything.

He didn't have to look far.

"Ian Knott," he whispered to himself. Ian Knott. Gord*ian* *knot.* Reef knot. Gordian reef. *It's just like my name.* He wondered if Gordon Reeve could smell him. He could smell Reeve. He was as close as a short walk, perhaps a flight of stairs. That was all.

"Where does Ian Knott work?"

"Mister Knott? He works part-time in the children's section. Nicest man you could hope to meet. Why? What's he done?"

"Is he in today?"

"I think so. I think he comes in for two hours at the end of the afternoon. Look, what's this all about?"

"The children's section, you said? That's downstairs, isn't it?"

"That's right." The guard was really flustered now. He knew trouble when he saw it. "I'll just phone down and let him . . ."

Rebus leaned across the desk so that his nose touched that of the guard. "You'll do nothing, understand? If you buzz down to him, I'll come back up here and kick that telephone so far up your arse that you really will be able to make internal calls. Do you get my drift?"

The guard started to nod slowly and carefully, but Rebus

had already turned his back on him and was heading for the gleaming stairwell.

The library smelled of used books, of damp, of brass and polish. In Rebus's nostrils it was the smell of confrontation, a smell that would remain with him. Walking down the stairs, down into the heart of the library, it became a smell of a hosing down in the middle of the night, of wrenching a gun away from its owner, of lonely marches overland, of wash-houses, of that whole nightmare. He could smell colours and sounds and sensations. There was a word for that feeling, but he could not remember it for the moment.

He counted the steps down, using the exercise to calm himself. Twelve stairs, then around a corner, then twelve more. And he found himself at a glass door with a small painting on it: a teddy bear and a skipping-rope. The bear was laughing at something. To Rebus, it was smiling at him. Not a pleasant smile, but a gloating one. Come in, come in, whoever you are. He studied the room's interior. There was nobody about, not a soul. Quietly, he pushed open the door. No children, no librarians. But he could hear someone placing books on a shelf. The sound came from a partition behind the lending-desk. Rebus tiptoed over to the desk and pressed a little bell there.

From behind the partition, humming, brushing invisible dust from his hands, came an older, chubbier, smiling Gordon Reeve. He looked a bit like a teddy bear himself. Rebus's hands were gripping the edge of the desk.

Gordon Reeve stopped humming when he saw Rebus, but the smile still played games with his face, making him seem innocent, normal, safe.

"Good to see you, John," he said. "So you've tracked me down at last, you old devil. How are you?" He was holding out a hand for Rebus to shake. But John Rebus knew that if he lifted his fingers from the edge of the desk, he would crumple to the floor.

He remembered Gordon Reeve now, recalled every detail of their time together. He remembered the man's gestures and his jibes and his thoughts. Blood brothers they had been, enduring together, able to read the other's mind almost. Blood brothers they would be again. Rebus could see it in the mad, clear eyes of his smiling tormentor. He felt the sea rushing through him, stinging his ears. This was it then. This was what had been expected of him.

"I want Samantha," he enunciated. "I want her alive and I want her now. Then we can settle this any way you like. Where is she, Gordon?"

"Do you know how long it is since anyone called me that? I've been Ian Knott for so long I can hardly bring myself to think of me as a 'Gordon Reeve.' " He smiled, looking behind Rebus's back. "Where's the cavalry, John? Don't tell me you've come along here on your own? That's against procedure, isn't it?"

Rebus knew better than to tell him the truth. "They're outside, don't worry. I've come in here to talk, but I've got plenty of friends outside. You're finished, Gordon. Now tell me where she is."

But Gordon Reeve only shook his head, chuckling. "Come on, John. It wouldn't be your style to bring anyone with you. You forget that I *know* you." He looked tired suddenly. "I know you so well." His disguise was slipping away, piece by careful piece. "No, you're alone, all right. All alone. Just like I was, remember?"

"Where is she?"

"Not telling."

There could be no doubt that the man was insane; perhaps he always had been. He looked the way he had looked on the days just before the bad days in their cell, on the edge of an abyss, an abyss created in his own mind. But fearful all the same, for the very reason that it was outwith any physical control. He was smiling, surrounded by colourful posters, glossy drawings, and picture-books, the most dangerous-looking man Rebus had met in his entire life.

"Why?"

Reeve looked at him as though he could not have asked a

more infantile question. He shook his head, smiling still, the whore's smile, the cool, professional smile of the killer.

"You know why," he said. "Because of everything. Because you left me in the lurch, just as surely as if we *had* been in the hands of the enemy. You deserted, John. You deserted *me*. You know what the sentence is for that, don't you? You know what the sentence is for desertion?"

Reeve's voice had become hysterical. He chuckled again, trying to calm himself. Rebus steadied himself for violence, pumping adrenalin through his body, knotting his fists and his muscles.

"I know your brother."

"What?"

"Your brother Michael, I know him. Did you know that he's a drugs pusher? Well, more of a middle-man really. Anyway, he's up to his neck in trouble, John. I've been his supplier for a while. Long enough to find out about you. Michael was very keen to reassure me that he wasn't a plant, a police informer. He was keen to spill the beans about you, John, so that we'd believe him. He always thought of the set-up as a 'we,' but it was just little me. Wasn't that clever of me? I've already fixed your brother. His head's in a noose, isn't it? You could call it a contingency plan."

He had John Rebus's brother, and he had his daughter. There was only one more person he wanted, and Rebus had walked straight into this trap. He needed time to think.

"How long have you been planning all this?"

"I'm not sure." He laughed, growing in confidence. "Ever since you deserted, I suppose. Michael was the easiest part, really. He wanted easy money. It was simple enough to persuade him that drugs were the answer. He's in it up to his neck, your brother." The last word was spat out at Rebus as though it were venom. "Through him I found out a little more about you, John. And that made everything easier in its turn." Reeve shrugged his shoulders. "So you see, if you turn me in, I'll turn him in."

"It won't work. I want you too badly."

"So you'll let your brother rot in jail? Fair enough. Either way, I win. Can't you see that?"

Yes, Rebus could see it, but dimly, as though it were a difficult equation in a hot classroom.

"What happened to you anyway?" he asked now, unsure why he was playing for time. He had come charging in here without a self-protective thought or a plan in his head. And now he was stuck, awaiting Reeve's move, which must surely come. "I mean, what happened after I . . . deserted?"

"Oh, they cracked me quite quickly after that." Reeve was nonchalant. He could afford to be. "I was out on my ear. They put me into a hospital for a while, then let me go. I heard that you'd gone ga-ga. That cheered me up a little. But then I heard a rumour that you'd joined the police force. Well, I couldn't stand the thought of you having a cosy life of it. Not after what we'd been through and what you'd done." His face began to jerk a little. His hands rested on the desk, and Rebus could smell the vinegary sweat coming from him. He spoke as though drifting off to sleep, but with each word Rebus knew that he was becoming more dangerous still, and yet he could not make himself move, not yet.

"It took you long enough to get to me."

"It was worth the wait." Reeve rubbed at his cheek. "Sometimes I thought I might die before it was all finished, but I think I always knew that I wouldn't." He smiled. "Come on, John, I've got something to show you."

"Sammy?"

"Don't be fucking stupid." The smile disappeared again, only for a second. "Do you think I'd keep her here? No, but I've got something else that will interest you. Come on."

He led Rebus behind the partition. Rebus, his nerves jangling, studied Reeve's back, the muscles covered in a layer of easy living. A librarian. A *children's* librarian. And Edinburgh's own mass murderer.

Behind the partition were shelves and shelves of books, some piled haphazardly, others in neat rows, their spines matching.

"These are all waiting to be reshelved," said Reeve, waving a custodial hand around him. "It was you that got me interested in books, John. Do you remember?"

"Yes, I told you stories." Rebus had started to think about Michael. Without him, Reeve might never have been found, might never have been suspected even. And now he would go to jail. Poor Mickey.

"Now where did I put it? I know it's here somewhere. I put it aside to show you, if you ever found me. God knows, it's taken you long enough. You've not been very bright, have you, John?"

It was easy to forget that the man was insane, that he had killed four girls in a game and had another at his mercy. It was so easy.

"No," said Rebus, "I've not been very bright."

He could feel himself tightening. The very air around him seemed to be getting thinner. Something was about to happen. He could feel it. And to stop it from happening, all he had to do was punch Reeve in the kidneys, chop him behind the neck, restrain him and bundle him out of here.

So why didn't he do just that? He did not know himself. All he knew was that whatever would happen would happen, and that it had been set out like the plan of a building or a game of noughts and crosses many years before. Reeve had started the game. That left Rebus in a no-win situation. But he could not leave it unfinished. There had to be this rummaging in the shelves, this find.

"Ah, here it is. It's a book I've been reading . . ."

But, John Rebus realised, if Reeve had been reading it, then why was it so well hidden?

*"Crime and Punishment.* You told me the story, do you remember?"

"Yes, I remember. I told it to you more than once."

"That's right, John, you did."

The book was a quality leather edition, quite old. It did not seem like a library copy. Reeve handled it as though he were handling money or diamonds. It was as though he had owned nothing so precious in all his life.

"There's one illustration in here that I want you to see, John. Do you recall what I said about old Raskolnikov?"

"You said he should have shot the lot of them . . ."

Rebus caught the under-meaning a second too late. He had misread this clue as he had misread so many of Reeve's clues. Meantime, Gordon Reeve, his eyes shining, had opened the book and brought out a small snub-nosed revolver from its hollowed-out interior. The gun was being raised to meet Rebus's chest when he sprang forward and butted Reeve on the nose. Planning was one thing, but sometimes dirty inspiration was needed. Blood and mucus came crashing from the suddenly broken bones. Reeve gasped, and Rebus's hand pushed the gun-arm away from him. Reeve was screaming now, a scream from the past, from so many living nightmares. It set Rebus off balance, plunging him back into his act of betrayal. He could see the guards, the open door, and he with his back to the screams of the trapped man. The scene before him blurred, and was replaced by an explosion.

The soft thump in his shoulder turned quickly to a spreading numbness and then to an intense pain, seeming to fill his entire body. He clutched at his jacket, feeling blood soak through the padding, through the lightweight material. Jesus Christ, so that was what it was like to be shot. He felt as though he would be sick, would faint clean away, but then he felt an onrush of something, coming up from his soul. It was the blinding force of anger. He was not about to lose this one. He saw Reeve wiping the mess from his face, trying to stop his eyes from watering, the gun still wavering before him. Rebus picked up a heavy-looking book and swiped at Reeve's hand, sending the gun flying into a pile of books.

And then Reeve was gone, staggering through the shelves, pulling them down after him. Rebus ran back to the desk and telephoned for help, his eyes wary for Gordon Reeve's return. There was silence in the room. He sat down on the floor.

Suddenly the door opened and William Anderson came

through it, dressed in black like some clichéd avenging angel. Rebus smiled.

"How the hell did you find me?"

"I've been following you for quite a while." Anderson bent down to examine Rebus's arm. "I heard the shot. I take it you've found our man?"

"He's still in here somewhere, unarmed. The gun's back there."

Anderson tied a handkerchief around Rebus's shoulder.

"You need an ambulance, John." But Rebus was already rising to his feet.

"Not yet. Let's get this finished. How come I didn't spot you trailing me?"

Anderson allowed himself a smile. "It takes a very good copper to know when *I'm* trailing them, and you're not very good, John. You're just good."

They went behind the partition and began to move carefully further and further into the shelves. Rebus had picked up the gun. He pushed it deep into his pocket. There was no sign of Gordon Reeve.

"Look." Anderson was pointing to a half-open door at the very back of the stacks. They moved towards it, slowly still, and Rebus pushed it open. He confronted a steep, iron stairwell, badly lit. It seemed to twist down into the foundations of the library. There was nowhere to go but down.

"I've heard about this, I think," whispered Anderson, his whispers echoing around the deep shaft as they descended. "The library was built on the site of the old Sheriff Court, and the cells which used to be beneath the courthouse are still there. The library stores old books in them. A whole maze of cells and passageways, leading right under the city."

Smooth plaster walls gave way to ancient brickwork as they descended. Rebus could smell fungus, an old, bitter smell left over from a previous age.

"He could be anywhere then."

Anderson shrugged his shoulders. They had reached the bottom of the stairs, and found themselves in a wide passageway, clear of books. But off this passageway were alcoves—the old cells, presumably—in which were stacked rows of books. There seemed no order, no pattern. They were just old books.

"He could probably get out of here," whispered Anderson. "I think there are exits to places like the present-day court-house and Saint Giles Cathedral."

Rebus was in awe. Here was a piece of old Edinburgh, intact and undefiled. "It's incredible," he said. "I never knew about this."

"There's more. Underneath the City Chambers there are supposed to be whole streets of the old city which the builders just built right on top of. Whole streets, shops, houses, roads. Hundreds of years old." Anderson shook his head, realising, as was Rebus, that you could not trust your own knowledge: you could walk right over a reality without necessarily encroaching on it.

They worked their way along the passage, thankful for the dim electric lighting on the ceiling, checking each and every cell with no success.

"Who is he then?" Anderson whispered.

"He's an old friend of mine," said Rebus, feeling a little dizzy. It seemed to him that there was very little oxygen down here. He was sweating profusely. He knew that it had to do with the loss of blood, and that he shouldn't be here at all, yet he needed to be here. He remembered that there were things he should have done. He should have found out Reeve's address from the guard and sent a police car round in case Sammy were there. Too late now.

"There he is!"

Anderson had spotted him, way ahead of them in such shadow that Rebus could not make out a shape until Reeve started to run. Anderson ran after him, with Rebus, swallowing hard, trying to keep up.

"Watch him, he's dangerous." Rebus felt his words fall away from him. He had not the strength to shout. Suddenly everything was going wrong. Ahead, he saw Anderson catch up with Reeve, and saw Reeve lash out with a near-perfect roundhouse kick, learned all those years ago and not forgotten. Anderson's head swivelled to one side as the kick landed, and he fell against the wall. Rebus had slumped to his knees, panting hard, his eyes hardly able to focus. Sleep, he needed sleep. The cold, uneven ground felt comfortable to him, as comfortable as the best bed he could want. He wavered, ready to fall. Reeve seemed to be walking towards him, while Anderson slid down the wall. Reeve seemed massive now, still in shadow, growing larger with each step until he consumed Rebus, and Rebus could see him grinning from ear to ear.

"Now you," Reeve roared. "Now for you." Rebus knew that somewhere above them traffic was probably moving effortlessly across George IV Bridge, people were probably walking smartly home to an evening of television and family comfort, while he knelt at the feet of this nightmare, a poor forked animal at the end of the chase. It would do him no good to scream, no good to fight against it. He saw a blur of Gordon Reeve bend down in front of him, its face pushed awkwardly to one side. Rebus remembered that he had broken Reeve's nose quite successfully.

So did Reeve. He stood back and swung a heaving kick at John Rebus's chin. Rebus managed to move slightly, something still working away inside him, and the blow caught him on the cheek, sending him sideways. Lying in a half-protective foetal position he heard Reeve laugh, and watched the hands as they closed around his throat. He thought of the woman and his own hands around her neck. This was justice then. So be it. And then he thought of Sammy, of Gill, of Anderson and Anderson's murdered son, of those little girls, all dead. No, he could not let Gordon Reeve win. It wouldn't be right. It wouldn't be fair. He felt his tongue and eyes bulging, straining. He slipped his hand into his pocket, as Gordon Reeve whispered to him: "You're glad it's all over, aren't you, John? You're actually relieved."

And then another explosion filled the passage, hurting Rebus's ears. The recoil from the gunshot tingled through his hand and his arm, and he caught the sweet smell again, something like the smell of toffee-apples. Reeve, startled, froze for a second, then folded like paper, falling across Rebus, smothering him. Rebus, unable to move, decided it was safe to go to sleep now . . .

# EPILOGUE

## I

They kicked down the door of Ian Knott's small bungalow, a tiny, quiet, suburban house, in full view of his curious neighbours, and found Samantha Rebus there, petrified, tied to a bed, her mouth taped shut, and with pictures of the dead girls for company. Everything became very professional after that, as Samantha was led weeping from the house. The driveway was hidden from the neighbouring bungalow by a tall hedge, and so nobody had seen anything of Reeve's comings and goings. He was a quiet man, the neighbours said. He had moved into the house seven years ago, at the time when he had started work as a librarian.

Jim Stevens was happy enough with the conclusion of the case. It made for a full week's stories. But how could he have been so wrong about John Rebus? He couldn't work that one out at all. Still, his drugs story had been completed, too, and Michael Rebus would go to jail. There was no doubt about that.

The London press came in search of their own versions of the truth. Stevens met one journalist in the bar of the Caledonian Hotel. The man was trying to buy Samantha Rebus's story. He patted his pocket, assuring Jim Stevens that he had his editor's cheque-book with him. This seemed to Stevens to be part of some larger malaise. It wasn't just that the media could create reality and then tamper with that creation whenever they liked. There was something beneath the surface of it all, something different to the usual dirt and squalor and mess, something much more ambiguous. He didn't like it at all, and he didn't like what it had done to him. He talked with the London journalist about vague concepts such as justice and trust and balance. They talked for hours, drinking whisky and beer, but still the same questions remained. Edinburgh had shown itself to Jim Stevens as never before, cowering beneath the shadow of the Castle Rock in hiding from something. All the tourists saw were shadows from history, while the city itself was something else entirely. He didn't like it, he didn't like the job he was doing, and he didn't like the hours. The London offers were still there. He clutched at the biggest straw and drifted south.

# ACKNOWLEDGEMENTS

The writing of this novel was aided hugely by the help given to me by the Leith CID in Edinburgh, who were patient about my many questions and my ignorance of police procedures. And although this is a work of fiction, with all the faults of such, I was aided in my research into the Special Air Squadron by Tony Geraghty's excellent book *Who Dares Wins* (Fontana, 1983).